Beside her, Jakob held out his hand. "Sarah?"

She ducked her head. "You don't have to."

"You'd rather not?"

At his hurt tone, she glanced up. Did he think she was rejecting him? "Oh, Jakob, I'm sorry." She extended her hand.

"Don't feel obligated." He dropped his hand to his side. "I don't want you to feel uncomfortable."

"I'd never feel uncomfortable holding your hand." Heat stung Sarah's cheeks. She sounded so overeager. "I just thought maybe you wouldn't want to hold mine."

Jakob's brow creased. "Why would you think that?"

"Never mind," Sarah mumbled. She lowered her head so Jakob couldn't see the love and joy shining in her eyes when he wrapped his hand around hers. She hoped he couldn't hear her thundering heartbeat or feel the tingling in her palm at his touch.

It had been years since they'd walked hand in hand, but every detail of his fingers, the pressure of his hand, had been imprinted in her memory. As they always had, their hands felt like the perfect fit.

A former teacher and librarian, **Rachel J. Good** is the author of more than 2,300 articles and forty books in print or forthcoming under several pseudonyms. She grew up near Lancaster County, Pennsylvania, the setting for her Amish novels. Striving to be as authentic as possible, she spends time with her Amish friends, doing chores on their farm and attending family events. Rachel loves to travel and visit many different Amish communities. Rachel enjoys meeting readers and speaks regularly at book events, schools, libraries, churches, book clubs and conferences across the country. Find out more about her at www.racheljgood.com.

GIFT FROM ABOVE

Rachel J. Good

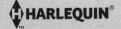

Recycling programs
for this product may
not exist in your area.

ISBN-13: 978-1-335-45491-1

Gift from Above

Copyright © 2019 by Rachel J. Good

Printed in U.S.A.

Chapter One

Although a brisk November wind rattled the kitchen window panes, Sarah Esh stood at the stove, wiping sweat from her forehead as she stirred a huge pot of applesauce. Everyone had been up since dawn preparing food for her sister Emma's upcoming wedding, and joy filled the room.

Mammi shuffled in from the *daadi haus*, her cheeks and nose reddened from the cold. Deep lines around her mouth and eyes revealed her arthritis was bothering her, but the determined set of her lips made it clear no one could convince her to stay in bed and rest. Sarah lowered the heat under the applesauce, set down the wooden spoon, and hurried to help her grandmother to the table.

"I'm perfectly capable of walking across the kitchen myself," *Mammi* griped as Sarah took her arm.

"Of course, you are, *Mammi*," Sarah soothed. "I just wanted to be sure that you didn't slip on the water we spilled earlier."

Mammi frowned. "And why wasn't that cleaned up immediately?"

"Oh, it was," Sarah hastened to assure her. "I was afraid it might still be slippery."

With a loud *humph*, *Mammi* sank onto the chair Sarah pulled out for her. Before her grandmother could insist on standing to help with wedding preparations, Sarah pointed to the loaves of bread on the table.

"Would you be willing to crumble the bread for filling?" It might not be easy for her grandmother to do that with her arthritic hands, but it was the least demanding task and didn't require standing or chopping. *Mammi* refused to admit any weakness and resented being catered to, so Sarah hoped this would keep her from feeling left out.

Her grandmother shot her an irritated look, indicating she knew Sarah was coddling her, but before Sarah turned away, *Mammi*'s features melted into sadness and then relief. Sarah longed to hug her grandmother and reassure her, but *Mammi* would only act prickly and deny any softer feelings.

Sarah returned to the stove to find Emma had taken over stirring the applesauce. Her sister inclined her head toward *Mammi* and smiled. Evidently Emma approved of Sarah's plan to keep *Mammi* involved without taxing her too much.

The back door banged open, and *Dat* entered the kitchen, whistling. As he passed Emma, he gave her a special smile, and Emma's already pink cheeks darkened to the color of the cherries they'd just prepared for the pies, warming Sarah's heart. After Emma's accident four years ago, *Dat* had been so gruff with her, but now peace had been restored, and Emma had gone back to being *Dat*'s favorite.

Sarah was relieved that harmony had returned to

the family, but she couldn't help feeling a slight pang. As the youngest of the three girls, she was often overlooked. Her oldest sister, Lydia, had always been *Mamm*'s helper. Lydia and *Mamm* were even closer now that Lydia'd had the twins, who were babbling in their playpen in the corner of the kitchen. Sarah was happy for her sisters, but sometimes she longed to be someone's favorite.

A knock at the front door startled them. Who would be calling at such an early hour?

Sarah hurried to answer. "*Gut...*" The cheery greeting died on her lips.

Jakob Zook stood on the porch. Her mouth went dry, and her heart rate tripled.

She barely managed to croak, "Jakob, what are you doing here?" Her words sounded so unwelcoming, her cheeks heated. "I'm sorry. I, um, *we* are always glad to see you. Come in, come in." Now she was gushing, and her face burned even hotter.

Jakob stared at the gray wooden boards of the porch rather than meeting her eyes. "Your *mamm* ordered a sewing cabinet for Emma's wedding gift. I finished it last night." His voice a monotone, he gestured to the driveway where his horse waited with a wagonload of wooden furniture. "I'm doing deliveries this morning. Should I bring it inside?"

"Yes, yes, of course." Sarah struggled to keep her tone neutral, but she still sounded overeager.

"Right." Jakob pivoted on his heel and headed toward the wagon.

His clipped response pierced Sarah's heart. She'd had a crush on him since childhood, but he'd chosen to court her sister Lydia. After Lydia rejected him and married someone else, he'd avoided dating, but even worse, he wanted nothing to do with their family. Sarah's heart ached for him. How painful it must be for him to deliver a wedding gift to their house.

Although he avoided looking at her or anyone else in their family, Sarah swiped at her face with a corner of her black work apron and tucked wayward strands of blonde hair under her work kerchief while his back was turned. If only she'd taken more care with her appearance this morning. Unfortunately, she'd thought of nothing but all the work they needed to finish.

Although Jakob had no interest in looking at her, she couldn't help staring at him as he crossed the lawn and leaned over the wagon. She admired his broad shoulders and the ripple of muscles under his blue work shirt as he lifted the cabinet. When he turned to head her way, she lowered her eyelids but peeped at him through her lashes, drinking in his glossy black hair under his straw work hat, his strong jaw tensed from the strain of carrying a heavy load, his confident gait as he strode toward her.

When he reached the porch, she pressed her back against the screen door to hold it open and clenched her hands into fists to keep from reaching out to touch him as he passed. Still, the fabric of his shirt sleeve brushed hers as he maneuvered the cabinet through the door, and Sarah's stomach fluttered.

"Where shall I put it?"

"Oh, um…" She couldn't let him carry it through the kitchen where he'd see Lydia and the *bopplis*. "Right here would be fine."

"In the living room?" Jakob stopped in the doorway

to the room. "I'm happy to carry it to wherever the gifts are being stored."

"No, no. That's all right. *Dat* and the boys will take care of it later."

"I don't want to make extra work for them." Jakob took a step toward the hall.

Sarah scurried over to block him. "Please," she begged, tears misting her eyes at the thought of him seeing her sister.

Their gazes met, and compassion flickered in his brown eyes—a softness he quickly shuttered. He turned abruptly and lowered the chest onto the rag rug in the center of the hardwood floor.

Sarah stepped closer and ran her hand over the satiny surface of the wooden cabinet. "It's beautiful."

"*Danke*." Although Jakob's voice was gruff, the tension lines on his face softened. "I'd better go. I have a lot of deliveries this morning."

Sarah hurried to open the door for him. "Does *Mamm* need to pay you?"

Jakob shook his head. "She stopped by last week with the money." After he stepped through the door, he added, "Tell Emma I wish her the best."

Sarah stood staring after him as his horse trotted off down the street. When he was nothing but a speck in the distance, she closed the door and slumped against it while memories of the past flooded her mind.

"Sarah?" *Mamm*'s sharp call startled her back to the house and the chores that needed doing. "Is everything all right?"

Sarah swallowed the lump blocking her throat. "It was Jakob," she responded. "He delivered Emma's gift. I had him set it in the living room."

"Wunderbar." *Mamm* headed down the hall. "I can't wait to see it."

Sarah stroked the wood, imagining Jakob's hands sanding and staining it. His strong, hardworking hands...

"Ach, it's even prettier than I expected." *Mamm* interrupted her thoughts. She wiped her hands on the dishtowel she carried before running a finger over the smooth seams and delicate details.

"I—I had him leave it here because, well—" She gestured in the direction of the kitchen.

"That was thoughtful of you." *Mamm*'s smile warmed Sarah. Praise did not flow freely in their house because their parents didn't want to encourage *hochmut*, so Sarah treasured the compliment.

"Well, we'd better get back to work." *Mamm* started down the hall. "I can't believe how much still needs doing before the wedding."

Thoughts of the upcoming ceremony brought tears to Sarah's eyes, and she swallowed a lump in her throat. With Emma's upcoming wedding, sadness often swept over Sarah because she'd never experience the joy of marriage and family the way her sisters would. Lydia had married at nineteen, the same age as Sarah was now, but the only man Sarah had ever loved had no interest in her. And with the way she felt about Jakob, it wouldn't be fair to marry anyone else. She'd have to be content caring for her parents and grandmother, teaching in the schoolhouse, and loving her nieces and nephews.

When she reached the kitchen, she tried to push aside her sadness, but Jakob's refusal to even look at her broke her heart. Cherry pies baking in the oven perfumed the steamy air, mingling with the aroma of tart apples and tangy cinnamon from the applesauce pot. The homey scents surrounded her, choking her, stinging her eyes. She had to escape before she put a damper on the festivities.

"I—I'm going out to cut a little more celery." Grabbing a sharp knife and snatching a cloak from the peg near the back door, she fled from the kitchen.

When she reached the garden, she pulled the cloak around her shoulders to ward off the chill. Then she adjusted her kerchief and took several deep breaths to calm herself.

Please, Lord, help me forget my own sorrow and concentrate on making Emma's wedding a happy occasion. Teach me to have a grateful heart for whatever You've called me to do. My only desire is to follow Your will.

Peace flooded her heart. She searched for the spade she'd used earlier. When she found it, she knelt in the celery patch, admiring the abundant crop her mother had planted in late June. Humming a song from the *Ausbund*, Sarah scraped away the dirt from a bunch of celery to expose the bottom of the stalks. She had just begun sawing below the stalks with the knife when a low buzzing drone came from above the distant fields.

A plane swooped close to the apple trees, so close she worried the pilot would crash. If he was headed for the nearby Lancaster small craft airfield, he'd never make it. Sarah dropped the knife and jumped to her feet, waving frantically toward the clear grassy hilltop behind the *daadi haus*. As if he'd seen her signal, the pilot banked toward the hilltop. Sarah exhaled a long breath. She'd diverted the plane to a softer landing place and saved the trees from being destroyed. She stood, hands clenched, as the plane slowed slightly. Then an orange wisp floated through the air. Something had fallen from the plane.

Before she could make out what it was, the plane soared off into the clouds. Her eye on the orange blob hurtling toward the ground, Sarah raced in that direction. The neon flash of color showed bright against the deep green backdrop of the pines before dropping out of sight.

When Sarah reached the hilltop, she stopped short. A man lay crumpled on the ground, heaps of orange cloth surrounding him. She clutched her hands together, fearful of approaching. She fainted at the sight of blood. She'd be no help to the parachutist if she passed out, but he needed assistance, and she was the only one here. He lay so still, could he be unconscious or, worse yet, dead?

Then he groaned. Sarah released the breath she'd been holding. He was alive.

"Are you all right?" she called.

"Do I look all right?" He let out a string of curses that blistered Sarah's ears. She longed to cover her ears, but that wouldn't be polite. Instead, she said a silent prayer for him and tried to tune out as much of his rampage as she could. The only positive thing about his swearing was he must not be too badly hurt. He was awake and conscious.

When he stopped for breath, Sarah moved closer and studied him, grateful for no sign of blood. Long strands of black hair that might have once been combed over the bald spot on his head flopped over one ear. With the way he was wriggling around and pounding the ground with his fists, he seemed to have no apparent injuries. Maybe he'd only had the wind knocked out of him.

His narrowed eyes and pinched lips made Sarah want to back away, but she asked gently, "Are you well enough to stand?"

"Would I be lying here on the ground if I could stand?" He glared at her as if she were a bug he longed to squish.

Sarah took a step backward so she was out of reach of his flailing arms. "I'm sorry, I just thought—"

"No, you didn't think. That's the trouble with most people. They start flapping their lips before they engage their brains."

Mammi often said something quite similar, although not in those words. Sarah hid a smile. She had a feeling this man might not appreciate being compared to her grandmother.

But if he was hurt, she had to help him. With a quick prayer for courage, she knelt beside him. "What seems to be the matter?"

His eyes squeezed shut, he clutched at his leg. "My *blankety-blank* leg."

Sarah tried to blot out the swear words. "I don't like to leave you alone here, but I'll run to call someone to help."

"Just use my phone." He moaned as he fumbled in his pocket, pulled out a cell phone, and held it out.

Sarah only stared at it.

"What's the matter with you, girlie. Take the phone." He shook it impatiently and thrust it toward her.

"How does it work?" Some of her friends, including Rebecca's boyfriend Abner, had cell phones, but she'd never paid attention to how they used them.

He snorted, but then a calculating look appeared in his eyes. "Hey, are you one of those Menno-whatevers?"

"Mennonites?" Sarah suggested.

"Yep, that's the ones."

Something about the way he was assessing her made Sarah want to back away, but she forced herself to stay still. "No, sir, I'm Amish."

"Amish? Well, well, well...this may work out even better." He squinted at her. "If you're really Amish, where's your head thingy?"

"My prayer *kapp*?"

"That's what you call those white thingies that stick out from the back of your head? You don't wear one?"

Sarah reminded herself he was hurt, so likely that was making him testy. "I wear a *kapp*, but not when I'm doing chores around the house. Then I usually wear a kerchief."

He waved toward the stand of trees behind her. "People don't want to see you in a regular old kerchief. Spoils the glamour."

People? What people? Sarah glanced over her shoulder to the spot he'd indicated, but the two of them were alone on the hilltop. Maybe he'd hit his head as well as his leg when he fell.

"Look, I need to get help. If your leg's hurt, our doctor makes house calls. I'm sure he'd come out here."

"No, wait. I'll make a call myself." After whisking a finger across his phone, he held it to his ear. "Slight change of plans here. Can't talk now, but I made a bad landing." He glanced over at Sarah.

She felt awkward listening in to a private phone conversation, and she itched to hurry back to the house to finish the wedding preparations, but she couldn't leave him here.

"I'll need a specialist. Helicopter one in if you have to. Be sure to tell him I broke my leg."

Sarah marveled at his confident tone. How could he possibly know his leg was broken? Perhaps he had medical training.

The stranger listened for a few minutes. "No, of course not. I guarantee this'll be even better. You'll see when you get here."

Stepping a short distance away, Sarah tried to divert her attention while he spoke, but his voice only grew louder.

"Right, right, you got it," he barked into the phone. "Whatever it takes. Make all the arrangements on throwaway phones, and be sure nobody discovers where I am. I promise this is going to be good, real good."

He was about to hang up when the voice on the phone squawked. "Oh, yeah, guess that would help." The stranger turned to Sarah. "What's your address?" He repeated it into the phone. Then he clicked it off.

"Someone's coming to fix my leg. I need you to go down and stand in front of the house to direct them up here when they arrive."

Sarah nodded and stood. "I'll go tell my family."

A sharp *NO!* exploded from his lips. "No one can know I'm here."

She stared at him. "But my family…"

"Are you hard of hearing? I said *no*."

Nibbling on her lower lip, Sarah tried to find a way to explain. "Everyone's probably wondering where I am. I only went out into the garden to cut some celery for my sister's wedding. They'll be—"

"Wedding? An Amish wedding?" His eyes bored into her. "Your sister, you say?"

"Yes," Sarah said hesitantly, a little unnerved by the intensity of his questions.

"When's this wedding?" he demanded.

"On Tuesday."

When the man lay back and closed his eyes, Sarah relaxed for a second, but then he began mumbling. "Today's Saturday, so there's what? Two, maybe three days?"

Unsure whether he was talking to her or to himself, Sarah remained silent. Then he sat up suddenly, grasping the phone. Again, after dancing his fingers across the screen, he lifted the phone to his ear.

"Send Paul here right away." Shooting a quick glance Sarah's way, he added, "I'll need an attendant because of my broken leg." He hung up abruptly.

"You don't know if your leg is broken yet," Sarah pointed out. "It might only be a bad sprain."

"Did you see my landing?"

Sarah scuffed a toe in the dirt at her feet. "No." All she'd seen was something orange plummeting through the sky.

"Then you don't know how hard I hit, do you? So maybe you should keep your trap shut." When Sarah gave him a blank look, he pinched his lips together with his fingers. "Like this."

He wanted her to keep quiet? She'd only been trying to be helpful, but evidently, he didn't appreciate that.

He squinted, grabbed his leg just above his knee, and moaned. This time his moan didn't quite sound genuine, but it wasn't her place to judge. Besides, as he'd pointed out, she had no idea of the intensity of his fall or his pain. Her heart went out to him. It wouldn't be easy to be hurt like this in a strange place with no family or friends around.

"If you're in pain, I can go for a doctor. Perhaps he can help until your specialist arrives."

The man's face reddened, and Sarah readied herself for another stream of curses, but he surprised her. He pinched his lips together for a few seconds and then blew out a long, exasperated breath.

"I'd rather wait for my doctor," he said in the calmest voice she'd heard from him yet. He looked up at her. "You people give sanctuary, don't you?"

Sanctuary? Sarah stared at him, trying to figure out what he meant.

"What? You've never heard the word?" The sharpness had returned to his tone. "Sanctuary is when you keep someone safe and their location a secret."

"Yes, I know what the word means, but…"

"What's with you and 'but'? You'd think you were a goat or something. Let them do the butting." He pointed to her family's farmhouse. "That your house?"

When Sarah nodded, his lips curled into a smile, one that reminded her of a fox, sharp and dangerous, and his eyes had the cunning look of a predator about to pounce. In a flash, that expression disappeared to be replaced by a pleading one. It happened so rapidly, she wasn't sure if she'd imagined the earlier expression.

"I need help. Sanctuary. Nobody can know I'm here. You have a large house. Two houses, it looks like, and a barn. Where can I hide that no one will find me?"

"I don't know if that's possible. With my sister's wedding, we have relatives and friends arriving from out of town. Every bedroom will be packed full." Ordinarily her younger brothers, Zeke and Abe, would give up their room for a guest, but they had already turned it over to uncles and cousins.

He sighed. "I guess it'll have to be the barn then."

"You won't get much privacy there with the cows and horses needing to be milked or fed. And *Dat* and the boys will be cleaning out the barn today for the wedding. The men and boys will gather out there on Tuesday."

He blinked. "You hang around in a barn during a wedding?"

"Yes, we do. At least the males do." Sarah tried to answer as sweetly as she could, hoping a soft answer would turn away his wrath, but so far everything she'd said seemed to stir up his temper.

He mumbled something under his breath that sounded like *What craziness!*

She may have misheard, though. Right now she had to figure out a way to help him. She pursed her lips. Then she brightened. "I have an idea." If this man's leg was broken, *Mammi* might agree. She couldn't promise to keep his presence a secret, though. "Just so you're aware, if you're staying with us, everyone in the family will know."

"You don't understand. Some men are after me and my secrets. They can't figure out I'm here or else…" He drew a finger across his throat. "If even one person discovers my whereabouts, I'm toast."

"Toast?"

"I'm dead. Get it?"

They'd kill him? Sarah pressed a knuckle against her mouth. She got it all right—his life was in her hands.

Chapter Two

His cell phone chirped, startling both of them. While he spoke to the caller, Sarah breathed deeply to calm her racing heart. If she told her family, would she be putting him in danger? But how could she not tell? It would be hard to hide his presence if *Mammi* agreed he could stay in the *daadi haus*. First, she'd have to get him there without anyone seeing him, then she'd have to make sure no one stopped by during the wedding. *Mammi* was the only one staying in the small house attached to their family home by a walkway, and she'd come to the main house for meals and wedding festivities. It might be possible, but it wouldn't be easy.

The man spoke into his phone. "I'll send the girl down to meet him." He listened for a few seconds before saying, "She says she has an idea. I've explained how important secrecy is, but I'm not sure she gets it."

Sarah did understand, but it would be *hochmut* to contradict him. Once he saw what she had in mind, he'd realize how hard it was to keep secrets in their busy, close-knit household. Even if her family found out he was there, she could count on them to protect him. Her community would too, given the chance, but she'd ask her family not to tell anyone else.

When the call ended, he turned to Sarah. "The doctor and my, um, attendant will be here in a few minutes. Go down to your front yard and direct them up here. And you said you'd figured out where I can stay?"

"I think so. I'll have to check with my grandmother first."

He squeezed his eyes shut with a pained expression. "I thought I made it clear no one can know I'm here." He said each word slowly as if talking to someone who was too dumb to understand.

"I know," Sarah said a bit tartly, but then regretted her tone. "I'm sorry. I didn't mean to speak so harshly. It's just that if you stay in the *daadi haus*, my grandmother will have to know because she lives there."

"Where's this dowdy-place you're talking about? I can't go traipsing about town where people will see me."

Sarah pointed down the hill. "It's the smaller house attached to the farmhouse. But why don't we see what the doctor says first? Maybe it's only a bad sprain, and you can go home. And I'll never mention I saw you. I don't even know your name."

"Oh, I have no doubt my leg's broken. And you'd know my name…" He paused. "Well, maybe you wouldn't, you being Amish and all." He thrust out his hand. "Name's Ha—Herman. Herman Melville."

Sarah shook his hand. "Nice to meet you, Mr. Melville. I'm Sarah Esh." She glanced down the hill. "Should I go down so I don't miss the doctor?"

A huge grin spread across his face. "Yes, why don't you do that?"

As she raced down the hill, Abe came barreling out the back door.

"Sarah," he yelled. "What are you doing?"

She slid to a halt. "A man got hurt up on the hill, and I have to meet the doctor."

"Everyone was worried about you. You weren't in the garden." Then he blinked. "A man hurt? I'll go call *Dat*."

Sarah held up a hand to stop his flow of words. "I don't have time to explain, but please don't bother *Dat*. The doctor will handle it." Barely pausing for breath, she rushed on. "Oh, and can you cut the celery for me? And ask *Mammi* to meet me in the *daadi haus* in a few minutes?"

She took off for the front yard, leaving Abe spluttering behind her.

A long black car inched along the road, stopping beside each mailbox. That must be the doctor. Sarah stepped out and waved. The car pulled up beside her, and two men hopped out of the back, one carrying a brown leather satchel and the other lugging a huge duffel bag.

"Mr. Melville is right up this hill." Sarah waved behind her, but instead of following her, the two men stared at her blankly. "You're the doctor who's coming to look at his leg, aren't you?"

The man holding the brown satchel started. "Melville? Leg?"

The other man jabbed him with an elbow. "Yes, we're here to look at *Mr. Melville's* leg."

"Oh, right. Mr. Melville has a broken leg. I'm Dr. Sanders. You must be the girl he mentioned." The older man with white hair pointed to the clean-cut, thirtyish man beside him dressed in jeans and a leather bomber jacket. "This is Paul, Mr. Melville's assistant."

Sarah beckoned for them to follow her. She didn't mean to be critical, but she wondered why a doctor would assume the leg was broken without examining the patient first. Mr. Melville must have been quite convincing over the phone. When Zeke had broken his leg, he'd been in a lot more pain, but maybe Mr. Melville was more stoic. And the doctor might change his mind after the examination. Sarah had to admit, she was hoping the diagnosis would be a sprain.

By the time they crested the hill, both men were panting. The younger one with the duffel bag sank to the ground and leaned against it. "Wow, carting this bag up here is more of a workout than going to the gym."

Dr. Sanders knelt beside Herman Melville. "What seems to be the trouble?"

"It's my leg, doc." Mr. Melville grimaced as the doctor slid a hand along his calf.

"I'm pretty sure this leg is broken, but I'll need to do a closer examination." Dr. Sanders glanced at Sarah. "Could you give us some privacy here?"

"Of course." Her cheeks hot, Sarah turned her back. Below her, *Mammi* headed toward the *daadi haus*. "I'll go down and check with my grandmother," she said over her shoulder. Then she tore down the hill and reached the house as *Mammi* pulled open the front door.

Mammi's brow creased. "Whatever is going on, Sarah? Abe went looking for you and returned with some garbled story about a hurt man."

"Let's go inside so I can explain." Sarah held the door as her grandmother hobbled through, and then she followed *Mammi* into the living room, where she recounted the story.

"So…" she finished, "I thought if his leg really is broken, perhaps we could get the hospital bed out of the shed and set it up for him." Following Emma's accident four years ago, they'd installed a hospital bed here in *Mammi*'s living room until her sister recuperated. The bed had been dismantled and stored in the shed ever since.

Mammi sat for a few minutes, looking thoughtful and pulling on her lower lip. "This certainly isn't the best timing, but God knew we'd need that bed again. I insisted on storing it when your *dat* wanted to sell it. And the Lord would expect us to care for a needy stranger."

"Thank you, *Mammi*. I knew you'd understand. I'll go tell them Mr. Melville can stay here if he needs to." Sarah jumped up and headed to the door.

"Mind you," *Mammi* called after her, "we can try to keep people from coming in here, but with all the wedding guests milling about, we can't guarantee someone won't see him."

"I've already warned him about that," Sarah said before hurrying back to the hill, where the three men were whispering together.

The lower half of Mr. Melville's body had been wrapped in a blanket, but the leg he'd complained about looked bulkier than the other one.

Dr. Sanders waved a hand toward it. "I'm afraid Herman was right about the leg being broken. He has two bad breaks, so he shouldn't be moved. I've put a cast on it, but he needs to be settled somewhere as rapidly as possible so the breaks can heal."

Sarah was amazed that Dr. Sanders had managed to

examine the leg and put on a cast in the short time she'd been with *Mammi*, but he was a specialist after all. "I'm so sorry to hear that, Mr. Melville. I hope you're not in too much pain. And forgive me for making light of your injuries earlier."

Herman Melville waved his arm around in a magnanimous gesture. "Apology accepted." Then he flapped a hand in Dr. Sanders's direction. "Doc here insists I shouldn't be moved or jostled. And as I mentioned, I need privacy."

Sarah suppressed a sigh. It looked as if they would be providing Mr. Melville with sanctuary, as he called it, until his leg healed. She mentally berated herself. The man was hurt and needed help. She shouldn't be complaining—even silently—about caring for a stranger. God had brought him into their lives for a reason. And perhaps they could be a blessing to him beyond assisting with his physical healing.

She glanced up to find all three men staring at her intently, questions in their eyes.

"I'm sorry," she said. "I checked with my grandmother, and she's agreed Mr. Melville can stay in the *daadi haus*."

A triumphant gleam lit Herman Melville's eyes. "Good, good. That should be perfect."

Sarah continued, "We even have a hospital bed in the shed, but I'll have to get *Dat* and my brothers to assemble it."

"A hospital bed?"

"My sister Emma was in a car crash several years ago. We needed it while she was recuperating."

Herman Melville's eyes narrowed. "Thought you people only drove buggies."

"We do, but she happened to be riding in a car."

Paul made a slicing motion with his hands, and Herman snapped his mouth shut. Paul stood. "Dr. Sanders and I can assemble the bed. No need to bother your family. As I'm sure Herman's explained, the fewer people who know he's here, the better."

As she led the two men to the shed, Sarah repeated, "I'll try to keep everyone away, but with two hundred guests coming, I can't promise privacy." So far, no one in her family had appeared to ask about the visitors, but perhaps they were all in the basement, setting up tables and chairs for the wedding meal.

Back in the *daadi haus*, *Mammi* supervised the men as they assembled the bed, and they deflected her many questions about Mr. Melville. The *daadi haus* only had a living room, kitchenette with small dining area, and bathroom downstairs. *Mammi*'s bedroom was upstairs. When Emma had used the bed, they'd placed it in the center of the living room, but the men rearranged the living room furniture to squeeze the bed in the back corner of the room, so it wouldn't be visible as people entered.

Before the men left to get Herman, Sarah asked, "How can you get him down the hill without jostling him?"

"Paul and I are both quite skilled at that," Dr. Sanders said. "Perhaps you could make sure no one from your family is watching while we do it."

Sarah scurried off to the kitchen. Everyone was so busy, they barely had time to listen to her explanation.

"Sarah," *Mamm* interrupted, "that pot's about to boil over."

By the time Sarah had the bubbling pot under control, Lydia was juggling the whimpering twins to take them up for naps, while *Dat* was prodding Zeke and Abe to finish setting up the tables in the basement so they could clean the barn. Sarah's conscience bothered her because she hadn't told them about the stranger, yet she was relieved she'd kept his secret. For now, at least.

Chapter Three

Just before everyone took a break for the noon meal, Sarah volunteered to take lunch over to *Mammi* and loaded the tray with an extra plate for Mr. Melville. Emma and *Mamm* were still setting the wedding tables in the basement while *Dat* and the boys washed up, so no one was around to question her. Doing something so clandestine troubled her, but her promise to keep Mr. Melville's presence a secret weighed heavily on her.

When she opened the door to the *daadi haus*, raised voices came from the living room. Before she could grab it, the storm door slammed shut behind her. At the loud bang, all noise in the other room ceased.

"Sarah?" *Mammi*'s voice quavered slightly.

"Yes, it's me. I'm so sorry I let the door bang. I was trying to balance the tray, and I wasn't fast enough to catch it."

"You nearly gave us all heart attacks." *Mammi* sounded like her old self again.

Sarah walked down the hall and entered the living room. She was surprised to see Paul leaning back in the recliner near the foot of the hospital bed, smiling and looking at home.

"Oh, I didn't realize you were here." Her face flushed hot as she realized how that sounded. "You're welcome, of course. I only meant I didn't know you were staying, or I would have brought three plates instead of two."

Paul waved a hand. "No worries. I'll be fine."

"Give him my plate, Sarah," *Mammi* said.

And despite Paul's protests, he finally agreed to accept the plate when *Mammi* insisted she'd eat in the kitchen later. He gobbled down every bite and thanked them both several times. Herman, on the other hand, picked at everything and turned up his nose at the forkfuls he did taste.

Mammi marched over to the bed. "Young man, in this house we never waste food. I noticed you didn't bow your head before you ate. Perhaps if you had, you'd be more grateful to God."

Herman almost choked on the small tidbit he'd put in his mouth. "God? What does God have to do with this s-slop."

Mammi bristled. "God has everything to do with it. All food comes to us through His bounty. In addition, hard work went into preparing that meal, so you will eat every bite on that plate and be thankful for it."

With a glare that would have quelled most people, Herman set down his fork. "I'll do whatever I *blankety-blank* please."

"Not in this house you won't. If your parents didn't teach you to respect your elders, I will."

Paul leaned farther back in the chair, grinning from ear to ear. "This ought to be good," he muttered.

Hands on hips, *Mammi* continued, "And furthermore, we don't use words like that in this house."

"Words like what?"

"Swear words." *Mammi* ticked them off on her fingers. "Absolutely no words about body parts. Or functions. And we do not take the Lord's name in vain, so don't say anything with God or Lord in it, unless you're praying." She gave him a stern look. "Something I'd highly recommend you do."

"How in the *blankety-blank* do you expect me to remember that?"

"If your *mamm* didn't see fit to wash your mouth out with lye soap when you were a youngie, I'd be happy to oblige."

"I just bet you would."

"We don't bet either."

"That figures." Herman sneered and tried to stare *Mammi* down but ended up being the first to lower his eyes. He fussed about the food, took minuscule bites, and threatened to send out for sushi. But with *Mammi* standing over him, watching him like a hawk about to swoop down on unsuspecting prey, he managed to finish every last bite.

"That's a good boy," she said as she took his clean plate.

"I'm not a two-year-old," he said through gritted teeth.

"Prove it by acting your age." *Mammi* returned his plate to the tray Sarah had carried in. "Oh, and mind your manners. *Danke* is in order when someone has done you a favor."

"What the…"

At *Mammi*'s raised eyebrow, he trailed off before finishing his sentence, and she beamed at him. He rolled his eyes. "So what's the danky-hanky or whatever?"

Paul leaned forward. "I took some German in high school. It means *thank you.* I think she meant you should thank Sarah here for the food."

Mammi sent Paul an approving look. "It seems your parents taught you some manners. But more important than thanking Sarah, he should bow his head and thank God."

"I don't believe in…"

Once again, she silenced him with a look. "It's prayer time. You can either say a silent prayer, or I can teach you The Lord's Prayer, the way we do for our little ones at bedtime."

Although he snorted, Herman dipped his head slightly and closed his eyes until *Mammi* said *amen.*

"Whaddaya know?" Paul laughed. "Never thought I'd see the day when you'd give up swearing and pray. Both in the same day."

Herman growled. "Shut the—" After a quick glance at *Mammi*, he amended it to *shut up.*

Paul's lips stretched so wide, Sarah wondered if his cheeks hurt. "Well, as you always say, 'When in Rome, do as the Romans do.' Here's your chance."

"I didn't mean it like this."

"But it applies, doesn't it? Up till today, you've always used it to excuse your vices. Now you can use it as an excuse for your good behavior."

Herman gave him a dirty look.

Mammi turned to Sarah. "I'd planned to go over to the house for dinner and supper, but I think I'd best stay here."

Sarah nodded. "I understand. I'll bring meals over for you."

"Don't bother bringing anything for me," Herman said. "I'll order my own." He pulled out his cell phone. "Oh—" He bit back a curse. "It's dead. You got a charger, Paul?"

As Paul dug through an outer pocket of his duffel bag, Herman held his phone out to Sarah. "Plug this in for me, would you?"

Sarah stayed by the door. "We don't have electricity."

"Of course you do. There's the outlet, and—" he pointed out the window "—those electrical wires connect with the eaves."

"I'm sorry, but we haven't paid for electricity for years. Not since my sister Emma recovered from her accident."

"I don't believe this. Stuck here without a phone. No electricity." Herman shook his head. "Paul, get the electric company on the phone and have them hook this place up. I don't care what it costs."

Sarah stood there in shock. "I don't think my *dat* would approve. He never wanted electricity in the first place."

"What your *dat*—I assume you mean your dad?—doesn't know, won't hurt him."

"Oh, no." Sarah hated to disagree with people, but she couldn't have a guest go against *Dat*'s orders. "Please don't do that."

Mammi cleared her throat. "Sarah is right. Her father would not want electricity. As a guest in this house, I'm afraid you'll need to follow the rules. In fact—" she strode over and snatched the cell phone from his hand "—I'll take charge of this so you won't be tempted."

"What?" Herman's mouth hung open, and he looked as if he'd been kicked in the gut by a horse. "You can't do that."

"I believe I just did." *Mammi* headed upstairs with the phone. "Don't worry, I don't intend to keep it. I'll return it when you're well enough to leave."

"But it's my property. I'll call my lawyer."

"A little hard to do when you don't have a phone," Paul pointed out drily.

"Let me borrow yours," Herman demanded.

"I'm not going to have you run down the battery by complaining to your lawyer. Coming here was your idea." Paul gave him a quelling look. "Did you forget that?"

Herman set his jaw and mumbled under his breath.

"I hope those aren't swear words," Paul said. "You might end up getting your mouth washed out with soap."

Chapter Four

That night Sarah was grateful to crawl into bed and snuggle under the warm Lone Star quilt *Mamm* had made for her. In the bed beside her, Emma slid under her matching quilt. Sarah was delighted to have her sister's company; the bedroom was lonely at night since both her older sisters had moved out. Until a few weeks ago, Emma had been staying with Lydia to help with the twins. It was nice having her here, if only for a short while.

After she finished her prayers, a heartfelt sigh escaped Sarah lips as she let go of all the pent-up tensions from the day. She had no idea what tomorrow would hold, but she was glad to turn all her worries and concerns over to God. She also realized that, despite the stress of keeping Herman's presence a secret, she'd appreciated the distraction, which had kept her thoughts from straying toward Jakob and her longing for the wonderful relationships her sisters had.

Emma wriggled around in bed and then rolled over to face her. "What's the matter, Sarah? You've been acting strangely all day."

Sarah sucked in a breath. Did her sister suspect that she was hiding Herman in the *daadi haus*?

Emma continued, "You looked so sad when you went out to cut the celery this morning. Is all the work for the wedding wearing you down?"

"Oh, Emma, no. Not at all. I'm happy to help. I want your wedding day to be as special as you are."

"You're such a sweet sister. I've always wished I had your peacemaking nature instead of my impulsiveness. If only I could be like you."

Emma's compliment made Sarah squirm. If only her sister knew how much Sarah wished to be in her place, planning a wedding with a man she loved. "If you were like me, you'd be destined to be an old maid instead of a bride."

The moonlight filtering through the window lit Emma's face as she leaned up on one elbow. "You're so pretty and kind, lots of men would be glad to marry you."

Sarah was sure Emma was exaggerating the "pretty and kind" part, and as for men wanting to marry her, she couldn't think of any who appealed to her. Besides, she had eyes for only one man.

"What's the matter?" Emma studied Sarah's face. "Surely you've had dates."

Sarah shook her head. "No, I've never been courted."

Emma sat straight up in bed, disbelief on her face. "No one has ever asked to drive you home after a hymn sing?"

"I didn't say that," Sarah mumbled. Various young men had offered, but she'd declined. It wouldn't be fair to lead them on when the only man she cared about was Jakob.

"Ah-ha, so they have." The triumph in Emma's voice turned to puzzlement. "Surely you didn't turn them all down?"

"What makes you think there was more than one?" Sarah wanted to steer this conversation in another direction before Emma hit on the truth.

"I knew it," Emma squealed. "I can tell from the way you asked that. You've had multiple offers. So who were they?"

Sarah lowered her eyes. "It doesn't matter. I wasn't interested in any of them."

"Any of them? How many were there?" Emma demanded.

"Maybe five or six," she muttered.

"Five or six?" Emma practically shrieked, but then she lowered her voice. "Most girls would be happy with one or two."

"I know." Sarah rolled over, her back to Emma. "I'm exhausted. We should sleep, so we'll be ready for all the visitors."

Tomorrow was an off-Sunday, which meant they wouldn't have church, but Sam's relatives would be arriving from Big Valley over the next two days.

"You're right. I can't wait for Sam's family to get here." The lilt in Emma's tone revealed how excited she was.

Sarah rolled back to face her sister. Emma was sitting up in bed, hugging her knees, a dreamy expression on her face. Sarah bit her lip and squashed the pang in her heart by reminding herself to put her sister's happiness before her own. "And you can't wait for Sam to arrive either," Sarah teased.

Her sister's face lit up. "Yes, it's been hard being

separated from him when I was used to seeing him every day."

The way Emma talked, it was as if she and Sam had been apart for weeks or months rather than three days. Following the usual custom in their *g'may*, Sam had moved into their house to assist with the wedding preparations, but yesterday he'd left for Big Valley to help his family get ready for their trip to Lancaster County.

"I still can't believe I'm going to marry Sam." Emma shook her head. "God is so good. When I think back to that day…"

Emma was referring to the day she'd discovered painful secrets about her past. Secrets she was positive would prevent her from ever marrying. Sarah had been able to do little to ease her sister's agony that day. Neither of them could have foreseen that less than a year later, Emma would be preparing for a wedding with the man she'd thought she'd lost forever. God was indeed good.

"My whole world fell apart that day." Emma's words were tinged with sorrow. "I never could have imagined God would bring such joy into my life."

Too choked up to speak, Sarah only nodded.

"You were such a comfort to me when I thought I'd never have a future, a relationship, a family. I hope someday I can help you in the same way." Emma sat straight up. "Wait a minute… We talked about you that day too."

Sarah wanted to cover her face, to hide from her sister's eager gaze.

Light dawned in Emma's eyes. "I was so upset back then, your words barely sank in. But I remember now.

You indicated you were in love with someone, but you thought it was hopeless. So who is he?" she demanded.

Sarah turned her head away, so her sister couldn't see the pain in her eyes. "It doesn't matter; he'd never consider me."

"You said he was older. By how much? Is he a widower?"

"Not that old. Please, can we drop this? I'd rather not talk about it." Thinking about it twisted the knife deeper into a wound that would never heal.

"No. I won't stop pestering you until you tell me."

Sarah sighed. When they were younger, Emma had always managed to worm secrets out of everyone. Knowing her sister, this questioning would go on all night.

Emma leaned toward her, eagerness in every line of her body. "Tell me. Please?"

What choice did she have? Emma would persist until she had her answer. "Jakob," Sarah mumbled. "Now you know why I have no chance."

Emma's eyebrows rose. "You mean Jakob Zook, who used to date Lydia?"

"*Jah*, and he's still in love with Lydia. He's not looked at another girl since she turned him down."

"Perhaps he's afraid he'll be rejected again."

"Who would do that? Anyone would be honored to have him."

"Especially you," Emma teased.

Tears welled in Sarah's eyes. How could Emma be so cruel? This wasn't a joking matter.

Emma reached out and squeezed her hand. "I'm not laughing at you. In fact, I think you and Jakob would be perfect together. I remember what good friends you were when you were young. You always looked up to him, didn't you?"

Sarah hugged her pillow to her chest. Yes, Jakob had been her hero since she was six years old, the day she'd found an injured kitten outside the barn. The sight of blood had terrorized her, so she'd stood, torn between her fears and picking it up to go for help. Just then, ten-year-old Jakob dashed around the corner, playing tag. Instead of scurrying past, he'd skidded to a stop.

"What's the matter?" he asked.

When she pointed to the kitten, he knelt to get a closer look. "Stay here with her, and I'll be right back."

He returned with a pail of water and some rags. "Don't watch," he warned as he bent over the kitten and sponged it gently.

Sarah kept her gaze averted from the kitten, which mewed in pain. Instead, she focused on Jakob's bent head and serious face as he murmured to the kitten, apologizing for hurting it more, but promising to help it get better. When he was done, he wrapped some clean rags around the wound, cradled the kitten close to his chest, and made it a little bed in the hayloft. Then he turned to her and wiped the tears streaming down her cheeks with the corner of a clean rag.

"Don't worry, Sarah, that kitten will live. The cut isn't too deep, and we can take good care of her."

Although the others teased him for playing with a little girl, Jakob ignored them and came every day to help her feed the kitten and change the rags. Often, he'd take her hand as they walked to the barn or put an arm around her shoulders as they squatted beside the kitten. He won her heart that day, and her feelings for him had only grown stronger with the passing years as she watched him mature into a handsome, upright, God-fearing man.

It had been a terrible blow when Jakob began courting her oldest sister. She'd been twelve, and much too young to date, when couples Lydia's age began pairing off. Jakob and Lydia had been one of the last. Until that fateful day Jakob had brought Lydia home in the courting buggy, Sarah had hoped he'd wait for her.

While he was dating Lydia, Jakob continued to tease her and treat her like a favorite younger sister. It hurt to know he thought of her as a child even though she was fourteen and he was eighteen. And as much as she loved Lydia and wanted the best for her—and who would be better than Jakob?—she suffered silently whenever her sister and Jakob spent time together during their year-long courtship. The older Jakob got, the stiffer and more formal he became. The fun-loving boy she'd known slowly disappeared to be replaced by a serious man. Yet her love for him never wavered.

Sitting across the table from him while he and Lydia studied the *Dordrecht Confession* for their baptisms had filled her with pain and pleasure. Sarah kept track of every day the couple spent together. Hearing that Lydia had refused Jakob's proposal had elated her, but that joy was crushed by her sympathy for Jakob's pain. He must have loved Lydia deeply because in the four years since their breakup, he'd never looked at anyone else. And he'd become even more sober after Lydia married another man. Sarah understood his loss and shared his pain, the pain of unrequited love.

She'd been so wrapped up in her memories, she hadn't realized Emma was waving a hand in front of her face and calling her name.

"Sarah? Sarah? Are you all right?"

No, she wasn't all right, and never would be—at least as far as Jakob was concerned.

"You really are besotted by Jakob, aren't you?" Emma gave her a sympathetic look. "You've been lost in daydreams ever since you mentioned his name."

"I'm sorry." Sarah tried to shake off the memories.

"I had no idea you felt this deeply about him."

Sarah wished she hadn't confided her feelings to Emma. Now her sister would pity her. If only there were a way to erase this conversation from Emma's mind. Sarah loved her sister, but Emma often blurted out things she later regretted.

Emma's eyes twinkled. "If you care about Jakob, why don't you give him some hints? If he's worried about rejection, you can ease his fears by letting him know how you feel about him."

Sarah gasped. "Oh, no, I couldn't. He's gone out of his way to avoid me since Lydia…"

"Maybe he was waiting for you to grow up."

"If that were so, he's had two years to let me know. He'll never get over his heartbreak." Just like she'd never get over hers.

"You never know until you try."

As much as Sarah wished for it, a relationship with Jakob was out of the question. He avoided her whenever they were in a room together. And she didn't blame him. Although she'd never be as pretty as her two older sisters, with her blue eyes and blonde hair, she looked enough like Lydia to cause him distress.

Tapping a finger against her lip, Emma gazed off into the distance for a while before her face brightened. "I have the best idea."

Sarah didn't like the gleam in Emma's eye, the one that always spelled trouble. "No, Emma." She had no idea what her sister was thinking, but she already knew she wouldn't like it.

"Yes, Sarah. I'll pair you two for the wedding dinner so you can convince Jakob you're perfect for him."

"Oh, no, please don't. Jakob can't stand being around me. He doesn't even talk to me."

"He will at dinner."

"Only because he's forced to be polite."

"Exactly, and you'll have a chance to remind him how charming you are, if he hasn't realized it already."

"You can't do that to him! It would be cruel."

"What's even crueler is watching my sister pine for someone when I can do something about it. I promised I'd pay you back for all your help."

"No, Emma, I'd rather give him up forever than let you torture him this way."

Emma smiled. "True love speaking. You care more about him than you do yourself. He's a lucky man to have such a devoted woman."

"Please, please don't do this."

"It's the perfect solution, Sarah. You'll see."

Sarah winced. Why didn't Emma understand? Lydia had hurt Jakob so deeply he still hadn't recovered. Although it would be torture to sit beside him, caring for him the way she did and knowing he'd never return those feelings, she dreaded the meal more for his sake. How awful for him to not only endure a wedding and see Lydia and Caleb together with their twins, but to be forced to sit beside the sister of the woman who had broken his heart.

Chapter Five

Sarah woke before dawn with dread churning her stomach. Last night's conversation with Emma washed over her. She had to convince her sister that pairing her and Jakob at the wedding was not a good idea. That worry almost overshadowed her apprehension about hiding Mr. Melville.

Emma was still sleeping, a beatific smile on her face, so she must be dreaming of Sam. Only two more days until they were husband and wife. Sarah pushed all thoughts of herself and her concerns from her mind. She needed to concentrate on making Emma and Sam's day special. With today being Sunday, they wouldn't do any major chores. Those that hadn't been completed this past week would be saved for tomorrow. Today was for spending time with guests and getting to know Sam's family.

Sarah slipped out bed, dressed quietly, did her hair into the usual bob at the back of her head, pinned on her *kapp*, and tiptoed to the door to avoid waking Emma. By the time she'd laid out the breakfast things and started preparing a tray for *Mammi* and Herman Melville, *Dat* and the boys were washing up. *Mamm* emerged from the bedroom as Sarah pushed open the back door. She hunched herself around the tray and kept her back to *Mamm*, so her mother couldn't see how much food she'd piled on two plates.

"Isn't *Mammi* coming over for breakfast?" *Mamm* asked.

"I—I don't think so." Sarah hoped her stuttering wasn't giving away her nervousness.

"She had lunch and supper in her room yesterday. Is her arthritis that bad?" The concern in *Mamm*'s tone added to Sarah's guilt. "I wonder if we should take her to the doctor tomorrow. It'd be a shame if she missed Emma's wedding."

"I'm sure she'll be fine for the wedding." Sarah wanted to reassure her mother, but she needed to get away before *Mamm* spied the overloaded tray.

"How would you know that?"

Sarah longed to say, *She's only staying in her house because we're hiding someone*, but she kept silent. Her throat ached with the unspoken truth. "I'll be right back," she said, letting the door slam behind her. She hoped *Mamm* didn't interpret that as rudeness. She was already harboring enough guilt.

The early morning air slapped Sarah in the face, reminding her that winter would soon be here. The maple branches stood stark and bare against the sky, but the oaks still clung to their russet leaves. Piles of crumpled brown leaves lay under the trees, and the wind whipped them about in a frenzied dance.

This time she knocked at the door of the *daadi haus* before entering. *Mammi* hurried to the door.

"Oh, it's only you," her grandmother said as she opened the door.

If she were Emma, Sarah would tease and ask *Mammi* who else she'd be expecting at such an early hour, but she only apologized for disturbing her and followed her to the living room, where loud snores filled the air. She set the tray down on the table and turned to find Paul asleep in the chair, head thrown back, and low-pitched snorting sounds coming from his open mouth. Herman's snores were loud enough to rattle the windowpanes, unless that was from the gusts outside.

"I didn't realize Paul would still be here." Sarah kept her voice low so she wouldn't disturb the sleeping men. "I'll go back and get another plate."

"Don't bother," *Mammi* retorted. "There's plenty here for three. Besides I'm planning to give Herman only a bite or two until he learns to appreciate every mouthful."

"Oh, *Mammi*." Sarah set the tray on the table.

"It's time that boy learned proper manners and respect for God."

Sarah wondered how Herman would like *Mammi* referring to him as a boy. He had to be in his late forties, maybe older. But if anyone could teach him manners and God-fearing behavior, it would be *Mammi*.

Herman flailed his arms and groaned in his sleep.

"Poor man," Sarah whispered. "He must be reliving the accident."

"Or more likely fighting his guilty conscience. Well, it's time he woke up."

"It's still early, *Mammi*. They're *Englisch*; they're probably used to sleeping later."

"Early rising will do them good." *Mammi* walked

over to the tray and banged a plate down with a loud thump.

Herman jolted upright, his arms thrashing. "What the—" He met *Mammi*'s glare and pinched his lips together. His jaw tightened, and his eyes narrowed. "Why are you disturbing people's sleep at the crack of dawn?"

"The crack of dawn? Look out the window. The sun's already above the horizon. Only the lazy are still in bed at this hour."

Paul yawned and stretched. "They get up with the roosters around here. Guess we'll have to get used to that." When Herman glowered, he laughed. "Look on the bright side. We won't be out all night partying and waking up with hangovers. A little healthy living never hurt anyone."

"Speak for yourself," Herman snarled.

While Paul teased and Herman groused, *Mammi* busied herself with the tray. She got out her mug and poured most of the coffee from one cup into it. She broke two tiny pieces from a cinnamon bun, cleared off a small plate, and put them in the center. Then she bustled over to Paul with a full plate.

"Umm, this looks delicious," he said, taking the plate with three cinnamon buns and two hardboiled eggs and accepting the cup of coffee.

Mammi smiled at him. "I hope you like your coffee black."

"Black's fine. Har—er, Herman and I often drink black coffee in the mornings. Helps with those hangovers I mentioned."

"Well, you won't have to worry about hangovers here." She turned to Sarah. "Why don't you serve Mr. Melville his?"

Sarah turned pleading eyes to *Mammi*. If it were up to her, she'd give him a full plate. With a loud *hmph*, *Mammi* crossed the room, picked up the plate with the two crumbs and the almost empty coffee cup, and strode over to Herman Melville's bed.

His eyebrows rose when he saw the plate, but when *Mammi* handed him the cup with less than a half inch of coffee in it, he exploded. "What's this? A joke?"

"No joke, Mr. Melville. You made it clear you were unhappy with the food last night and could barely swallow a bite or two without someone standing over you. I have better things to do with my time than supervising your eating. So I'm giving you what I think you can eat without my assistance."

Herman's mouth hung open.

"Maybe I miscalculated?"

Giving her a grumpy look, he snapped, "I'll say you did."

"All right then." *Mammi* picked up one of the crumbs, popped it into her mouth, and held out the plate with one crumb.

Herman's eyes popped open even wider, and a red flush began at his neck and crept up his cheeks.

Paul was laughing so hard, he choked. He thumped a fist against his chest to stop the coughing fit, but his peals of laughter grew louder as Herman's face turned scarlet and his mouth opened and closed, but no words came out.

Sarah felt sorry for the man. "Mr. Melville can have my cinnamon rolls if he'd like them."

"We can't afford to waste food," *Mammi* said. "Unless Mr. Melville agrees to eat every bite without complaint…"

"All right, all right." Herman Melville held up his hand. "I promise to eat whatever you give me without complaining."

"And to thank God for each bite," *Mammi* added.

Herman rolled his eyes heavenward.

"*Wunderbar.* You're looking in the right direction."

Fists clenched, Herman hissed out a breath through his teeth. When he opened his mouth, looking as if he was about to explode, Paul wagged a finger at him.

"Temper, temper. Remember, no swearing."

Glaring at Paul through slitted eyes, Herman spat out each word. "All right. Just get the prayer over with."

Mammi patted his shoulder. "Good. That's another move in the right direction."

He flinched away from her touch.

"Ordinarily we pray silently, but I'll pray aloud using words that should be familiar to you." *Mammi* bowed her head and recited The Lord's Prayer.

When she was done, Paul swiped his eyes with the back of his fist. Sarah wasn't positive, but his eyes seemed to glimmer with tears.

Mammi nodded for Sarah to bring the full plate to Mr. Melville, and she handed him her full mug of coffee. "I'll join the family for breakfast if you two think you can behave."

Paul nodded. "Don't worry. I'll make sure we're both on our best behavior while you're gone."

"I'm counting on you," *Mammi* said as she took Sarah's arm and headed for the door. After they were outside, *Mammi* shook her head. "Something's not right with those two, but I'm not sure what."

Sarah had a similar feeling, but as they entered the kitchen, she brushed aside her misgivings and concentrated on breakfast and on preparing for the guests who'd soon be arriving.

Mamm whispered to Sarah that she was relieved *Mammi* was well enough to attend the wedding. Sarah longed to share the truth about the men in the *daadi haus* and the real reason for *Mammi*'s absence from the meal table, but she stayed silent. Stomach roiling at her duplicity, she turned away to clear the breakfast dishes. Was it right to keep such a secret from *Mamm* and *Dat*?

She argued with herself as she washed the dishes but remained undecided. *Mammi* returned to the *daadi haus* to babysit the men and came back with the empty tray. The guests must have enjoyed their meals. Even Herman had left no crumbs on his plate.

As she washed the dishes, Sarah tried to think of a way to keep Emma from talking to Jakob. Maybe she could discuss it with Sam. Once he understood the situation…

Emma's joyful squeal indicated that Sam had arrived. Sarah dried her hands and hung up the dishtowel before joining her family in the living room. As Sam's buggy came to a halt in the driveway, Emma threw open the door but stood on the porch, hands twisting the folds of her skirt, while Sam helped his mother from the buggy. Sarah could tell her usually exuberant sister wanted to fly out the door and hug Sam, but she was holding herself back.

When Sam's eyes met Emma's, all the love in them made Sarah's heart melt. She'd love to have a man look at her that way. And not just any man. Only *one* man would do.

The day passed in a flurry of greetings and conversations. Sarah slipped out before each meal to bring trays to the *daadi haus*, and *Mammi* left the men alone and joined the family for meals. As Sarah passed Herman's bed to collect the tray after dinner, he gripped her wrist.

"Who made those cinnamon buns this morning?" he demanded.

Sarah tried to twist away, but he held firm. "I—I did."

"You're scaring her," Paul said, and Herman let go of her arm.

As Sarah backed away, he asked, "Do you cook other things as good as that?"

She shrugged. "All *Mammi*'s recipes are good."

"So that was your grandmother's recipe?"

The eager light in his eyes made her uncomfortable, but he was interested in recipes, not her, so she tried to be polite. "Most of the things we make are from *Mammi*'s recipes. She's a wonderful *gut* cook."

"Hmm…" Herman looked at Paul. "I have an idea."

Paul's usual grin widened. "I bet I can guess what it is." Then he glanced at *Mammi*, who was just entering the living room. "Except we can't bet."

Sarah picked up the tray and hurried off. She'd be careful to stay away from Herman from now on. Until now, she hadn't thought about the possibility that the men might be dangerous. She hoped she wasn't leaving *Mammi* in any danger. Then remembering how *Mammi* had gotten the better of Herman, she smiled. Her grandmother would put him in his place. And Paul seemed nice enough. Still, she murmured a prayer that God would protect *Mammi*.

When bedtime came, Emma showed Sam's sisters up to their bedroom, where each girl would have one of the three beds. Emma and Sarah were supposed to sleep in the *daadi haus*, but Sarah suggested Emma might be more comfortable on the living room couch. She breathed a sigh of relief when her sister agreed.

Several friends and relatives were hosting other members of Sam's family. Sam and his brothers were staying at the Zooks' house. Sarah hoped Sam wouldn't ask Jakob about pairing up with her at the wedding. Her stomach in knots, she retreated to the *daadi haus* to sleep upstairs. Just before she fell asleep, Sarah whispered a prayer that God would spare Jakob any pain during Emma's wedding, and she asked for forgiveness for deceiving her parents.

The next morning Sarah woke early, dressed, and tiptoed from the *daadi haus* to start breakfast, a casserole made of eggs, shredded bread, cheese, and bits of sausage. She had just finished her chores and was checking the bubbling casserole in the oven when *Dat* came through the kitchen after doing the morning milking. Abe and Zeke bounded past a few minutes later.

"Don't slam the door," she warned the boys. "Some of our guests may still be sleeping." Although the two men in the *daadi haus* were likely the only ones still abed.

While they washed up, Sarah pulled the smaller casserole from the oven a little earlier than the larger one and set it on a tray with plates, juice glasses, and cups of coffee. Then she hurried to the *daadi haus* and handed the tray to *Mammi*.

"Breakfast will be ready in about ten minutes," Sarah told her and rushed toward the door. "Oh," she said over her shoulder, "I hope you'll give Mr. Melville a full plateful."

"We'll see," *Mammi* retorted. "With all the work needing to be done today and tomorrow, I won't be able to keep much of an eye on them, though. I hope that won't be a problem."

Sarah hoped not too.

After breakfast, everyone scattered to do chores or work on wedding preparations. Sam and his brothers joined *Dat* in the barn to clean. After lunch, *Dat* asked Sarah to rake the yard before the wedding trailer arrived with the dishes. The other women went to the basement to arrange bunches of celery and fruit into centerpieces.

Grateful to be outside in the brisk fall air after spending the morning in the heated kitchen, Sarah inhaled a deep breath. She'd raked several piles by the time her brothers got home from school. They jumped in the leaves, rolling in them, tossing them, and throwing handfuls at each other as if they were four and five instead of ten and eleven.

Sarah hated to scold them when they were having so much fun. "Zeke! Abe!" she called, "I need your help."

Reluctantly, they stood and brushed themselves off. She handed Zeke the other rake and asked Abe to bag the piles under the tree. The three of them worked steadily for about an hour before a silver car pulled into the driveway. More of Sam's relatives must have arrived. Sarah handed Abe her rake, straightened her kerchief, and went toward the car, but then stopped in surprise.

"Kyle?" What was Emma's ex-boyfriend doing here?

The tall blond *Englischer*, who'd emerged from the car, held out his hand. "Sarah, right?" When she nodded, he continued, "Caleb told me he and Lydia were coming here for Emma's wedding."

"Oh…" She exhaled in relief. Of course. She'd almost forgotten he was Caleb's brother. "I'll run and get Caleb. I think he's in the barn helping *Dat*."

Kyle shuffled his feet. "Actually I'm not here to see Caleb. I, um, wanted to talk to Emma."

"Emma?" She could think of no reason why he'd need to see her sister, but how did she politely ask him to come back another time? "I hope you haven't traveled far. Everyone's really busy with wedding preparations, so later in the week might be better for her. She and Sam will be staying here until Friday." Then they'd be taking off to visit Sam's relatives on the weekend to collect their wedding gifts.

Kyle winced at Sam's name. "I need to see her before the wedding. I have something urgent to ask her." He looked on the verge of tears. "I drove all the way from North Carolina."

Sarah studied the dark circles under his eyes. "That's a long trip. You must be tired. Come inside and sit down. Can I get you something to eat?"

"No, thank you. All I want to do is talk to Emma. In private," he added, his eyes pleading with her to understand.

Sarah could think of no spot for privacy amidst the pre-wedding chaos. "I'm not sure where you can go. Perhaps the *daadi haus*?" She gestured toward the window, but then her outstretched arm froze in place.

Not only had she realized her mistake, but inside the window, the blinds were crooked, and a video camera was pointing straight at them.

Chapter Six

Sarah dashed across the lawn toward the *daadi haus*, Kyle at her heels.

The camera lens disappeared, and the blinds fell back in place.

By the time she reached the porch, she was panting. She yanked open the doors but held an arm out to stop Kyle from entering. "Please stay here."

Kyle ignored her and followed her down the hall.

"I've got snowmen," Herman announced as she raced through the doorway.

Paul glanced up from the wooden chair he'd pulled beside the hospital bed. "Hey, Sarah, you been out jogging or something? You're wheezing."

Sarah studied their faces and the room. No sign of a camera anywhere, and they'd turned the meal tray into a card table. Cards and plastic circles were lined up across its surface. It looked as if they'd been playing for a while. Had what she'd seen in the window only been a trick of the light?

"We're playing Texas hold 'em." Paul smiled. "Don't worry, we're only fake betting. Your *mammi* put the fear of God into us. You and your boyfriend there want to join us?"

"He's not my boyfriend. He's my sister's…" Sarah stopped midsentence; she didn't want to hurt Kyle's feelings by calling him an ex-boyfriend.

Paul raised his eyebrows. "Thought she was getting married. You married gals allowed to have boyfriends?"

"*Ach*, no." He'd misunderstood. Sarah was so flustered she couldn't think straight. "He's a—"

"A friend," Kyle finished for her.

She glanced at him gratefully, but then turned to meet Herman's angry eyes.

The rage on his face as he flicked his head in Kyle's direction made Sarah's blood run cold. "We had an agreement."

"I—I'm sorry. I asked him to wait, but when we saw…" She was beginning to doubt whether she'd actually seen anything. She glanced back over her shoulder at Kyle. Had he spotted the video camera too?

He must have misunderstood her eye signal as a call for help, because he moved beside her, standing at an angle that partially blocked her from Herman's view. "She didn't have a choice. I followed her."

"Get him out of here." Herman's voice was low but deadly.

Paul waved a hand in the air. "Relax. I've told you. You have nothing to worry about. The Amish are a closed community. They don't reveal anything to outsiders."

Kyle stared from one to the other, his eyes brimming with questions. Ignoring the tension in the room, he asked, "So, either of you own a video camera?"

Paul's expression remained neutral, but Herman said

sourly, "I've got one on my phone, but—" he glared at Sarah "—it's useless, unless someone sees fit to hook up the electricity."

Sarah released a pent-up breath. Kyle had seen the camera too. She hadn't been mistaken. But how had Paul and Herman had time to set up a complicated card game while she was running across the lawn? And they both looked so innocent. Her gaze rested on the huge duffel bag beside the recliner. That was large enough to hold camera equipment. If only she were brave enough to peek inside.

Paul picked up the tray. "I need a bathroom break. I'll set this over here while I'm gone—" he balanced the tray on a nearby end table "—and I'll trust you to keep Herman from cheating."

Herman locked gazes with Kyle. "You have no business here. Get out," he said between clenched teeth.

Kyle stayed where he was. "I believe we're both guests here, so it's up to Sarah to decide who stays or leaves." His calm, even tone soothed her.

Sarah admired his ability to defuse a volatile situation while her nerves were ragged. As a med student, he must be used to calming fearful or angry patients. But she could depend on her source of inner strength.

Lord, give me Your wisdom and peace. Show me what to say and do.

When Paul strolled back into the room, Kyle said, "So, Sarah, you never introduced me to your guests."

Introduce him? While she was trembling at the fury on Herman's face? After she'd promised not to tell anyone about Herman? *Please give me courage, Lord.*

"Sarah?" Kyle stepped closer. "Are you okay?"

"I'll be fine," she croaked. "I just don't know if…"

The words stuck in her throat. She reminded herself that she had prayed for courage, and God was here with her. She had no need to fear. Taking a deep breath, she performed the introductions.

Kyle's eyebrows shot up when she introduced Herman Melville, but he only murmured, "Nice to meet you."

But Herman was not as pleasant when Sarah mentioned Kyle's name. "Kyle. Doesn't sound like an Amish name to me."

"It's not, sir."

Herman's face darkened. "He's not Amish," he barked at Paul, as though blaming him. Then he pinned Sarah with a scowl. "This is all your fault. If he mentions to anyone that I'm staying here, I'll track him down and—"

Paul interrupted. "This kid has no idea what's going on. And I'm sure he won't say anything. After all, why would he gossip about a stranger who's stuck in bed recovering from a broken leg." The semi-friendly smile he sent Kyle's way had a hidden warning underneath that was almost more frightening than Herman's blustering.

Kyle held up a hand. "I don't know anything and don't want to know anything. I'm out of here. All I came to do was talk to Emma. Believe me, I won't mention this to anyone." He picked up the tray and carried it toward the bed. "Why don't you go back to your card game and forget I was ever here?"

As he neared the bed, Kyle tripped, and the tray went flying. He grabbed for the bedrail, but instead managed to grab a handful of blanket, yanking it off Herman's lap. "I'm so sorry," he said as he righted himself and began rearranging the blanket back over Herman's broken leg.

Herman batted his hands away. "You—you—" He looked as if he were ready to throttle Kyle.

"I hope I didn't hurt your leg more," Kyle's honeyed tones of concern sounded almost mocking. "And I apologize for messing up your game. I hope you weren't winning."

Paul's lips thinned into a grim line. "I suggest you leave *now*."

"Don't worry, we're going." Kyle motioned for Sarah to precede him into the hallway. This time she covered her ears as Herman let loose with a volley of curses that followed them outside. Sarah prayed none of the guests were within hearing distance.

After he closed the door behind them, Kyle placed a hand on Sarah's arm. "I'm really sorry I stirred up such a hornet's nest. I'm afraid you're the one who'll get stung."

"*Ach*, you couldn't have known. I should have stopped you from entering."

Kyle sighed. "And I only made it worse by pulling off that blanket, but I had to know."

"You did that on purpose?" Sarah's eyes widened. "It looked like an accident."

"Good. I was afraid they might have suspected." He looked over his shoulder as if expecting the door to burst open. "Why are they here?"

"Mr. Melville broke his leg in two places in a parachuting accident. He can't be moved until it heals, so he needed a safe place to stay. Some men are after him, and that's why he doesn't want anyone to know he's here."

Kyle tilted his head as if he didn't believe her. "I don't

know what he's up to, but that man's a fraud. And his name—Herman Melville. Is that a joke?"

"A joke? What do you mean?"

His voice rough, Kyle snapped, "That's the name of a famous author. A dead author."

"Maybe he was named after the author."

Kyle blew out an exasperated breath. "I doubt it. That's not his real name. It's an alias. He's not who he's claiming to be. But who is he, and why is he here?"

Sarah shook her head. "Whatever his name is, he needs help. He can't get around on a broken leg."

"That's another thing," Kyle burst out. "That leg's a fake too. He has a walking cast. There's no reason why he can't get out of bed."

"But he said…"

Kyle interrupted her. "Do you believe everything everyone says?"

"Of course. Why wouldn't I?"

"Because people lie."

"It's not my place to judge."

Kyle's breath hissed out between his teeth. "Your naïveté is going to get you in big trouble someday. Watch out for this man. He's not who or what he's claiming to be. I just hope he doesn't do something to hurt you or your family."

"I'm sure his intentions are honorable."

"And I'm equally sure they're not." Kyle spun on his heel and stalked toward the front door. "Don't say I didn't warn you."

"Kyle, wait, please." Sarah hurried after him. "I didn't mean that I don't believe you."

The hard look in his eyes softened as he studied her

face. "I know you mean well and want to think the best of everyone. Those are admirable qualities, but—"

Now it was Sarah's turn to interrupt. "There's nothing admirable about it." To think otherwise was *hochmut*. "It's how God would have us treat others."

The admiration glimmering in Kyle's eyes made her uncomfortable, so Sarah lowered her gaze.

"I hadn't realized how much you look like your sister," he said. "But when your eyes were shining just now, I saw a flash of Emma." He swallowed hard. "Please can you let her know I want to talk to her?"

"I don't know if it would be wise."

"Please? It won't take long. I only have one question for her."

Reluctantly, Sarah plodded toward the kitchen.

Kyle remained on the porch of the *daadi haus*. "Thank you so much. I'll wait here for her."

Sarah pushed through the bustle in the kitchen, searching for Emma. Everyone she asked pointed her to the basement, so she headed downstairs to see the room below transformed. Squeezing in enough long tables to seat the guests meant narrow spaces between the benches, but no one would mind. Although their large basement had bare cement walls with tiny casement windows, the tablecloths and centerpieces made the room look lovely and festive.

"Emma," Sarah called, "you're needed outside."

Her sister dropped the roll of ribbon and scissors. "The wedding wagon's here early." She bounded up the stairs.

"Wait," Sarah said. "It's not the wedding wagon."

Emma turned, a look of puzzlement on her face, but then she beamed. "Oh, Sam wants to see me."

Sarah shook her head. "No, not Sam. Someone else."

Her sister frowned. "Why so mysterious? Who is it?" She continued up the steps. "Is it a surprise?"

It would be a surprise, all right. Before Sarah could explain, Emma raced through the kitchen and yanked open the door. Her whole body slumped when she saw Kyle.

"What's he doing here?" she said, her words quiet, but desperate.

"He drove all the way here to talk to you."

"Oh, Sarah, how could you do this to me?" Emma's fingers dug into her arm.

"I'm so sorry. I didn't want to, but…"

Emma let go of Sarah's arm and yelled across to Kyle, "What do you want to talk about?"

Kyle squeezed his eyes shut for a second. "I was hoping we could go somewhere more private."

"I'm getting married tomorrow, Kyle. That wouldn't be appropriate."

"Could you come over here, so I don't have to shout?"

With a loud huff, Emma marched past Sarah and up the walkway. Eager to escape, Sarah opened the kitchen door. It wasn't even lunchtime yet, and she'd had more stress in one morning than she usually faced in months—or years.

"Sarah, wait," Emma called after her. "Maybe you should stay here."

"I don't think so. Kyle wants to talk to you alone."

"Can you hear what we're saying if you stand there?" Emma lowered her voice to a conversational tone and said something to Kyle.

Sarah shook her head.

"So stay there and be our chaperone. If you can't hear, that will be enough privacy."

The pained look on Kyle's face showed he didn't approve of the plan, but if Emma wanted her to watch, Sarah would oblige. Although she couldn't hear, Kyle leaned toward Emma, every line of his posture revealing how much he still cared for her. When he reached for her hands, Emma pulled away and tucked them behind her back.

The closer Kyle came, the farther Emma retreated. He held out his hands in a pleading gesture. Sarah couldn't bear to watch the pain on his face, so she averted her eyes, until Emma's explosive NO! rang through the air. Tears streaming down her face, Emma raced toward Sarah, brushed by her, and slammed the door.

Kyle gazed after Emma, his eyes wet with tears, and then he stumbled down the steps.

Sarah should go after her sister and comfort her, but Kyle appeared so dejected, and he'd come all that way. He looked in no shape to drive back to college. "Kyle, wait."

Head down, Kyle ignored her, so she chased after him. "Do you want me to get Caleb for you? I'm sure he'd want to see you."

"I don't want to see anyone right now." He kept his back to her and kept walking.

"If you wait a few minutes, I can pack some food for the road. I don't like to think of you driving all that way when you're upset. Do you want to come in for a while? Or sit on the porch?"

"No, I just want to get out of here, to drive away and try to forget." His voice broke. "I'm sorry I upset her, but I had to ask. I couldn't go through life not knowing."

"Not knowing what?" Sarah asked gently.

"Whether or not she still loved me."

"Oh, Kyle, I'm sorry."

Kyle whirled toward her. "What are you sorry about? You barely even know me."

"No, but I know how much it hurts to love someone who's in love with someone else."

"Then I feel sorry for you too, Sarah. It sucks." He reached the car, yanked open the door, and slid into the driver's seat. Then he looked up at her. "Remember what I said about those guys and be careful."

"I will. And you be careful driving."

"I always am *now*. Perhaps if I'd been cautious back then, I'd still have Emma."

Sarah's heart ached for Kyle. She wished he and Emma had never been in that terrible accident, but she was grateful her sister hadn't married an *Englischer*. God had used that car crash to bring Emma home and back to the faith.

As Kyle took off down the driveway, Sarah prayed for his safety on the journey and, even more importantly, that Kyle would find his way to God.

Chapter Seven

Sarah hurried into the house to look for Emma. Her sister should be joyful today rather than teary-eyed. If only Kyle hadn't arrived to upset her. Emma lay face-down, sobbing, on the sofa.

"I'm so sorry, Em. I wouldn't have let him talk to you if I'd known."

Emma waved a hand. "Not your fault." The fabric of the couch muffled her words. "Why did he have to come and remind me of the past? I didn't want to hurt him, but I've put all that behind me. He needs to move on, find someone else."

"I wish I'd asked Caleb to talk to him instead."

Her eyes overflowing with tears, Emma lifted her head. "No, that wouldn't have worked." She heaved out a shuddering breath. "He had to hear it from me. I doubt he'd have believed anyone else. But to see his face crumple like that… My heart aches for him."

"Mine too."

"Oh, Sarah, you feel the same pain, don't you?" Emma dashed away her tears with the back of her hand. "I have no business crying the day before my wedding.

I'm so grateful for Sam, and I want you to be as happy as we are."

Sarah reached for her sister's hands. "I love you for caring about my well-being when you're so busy with wedding plans." Maybe now she could convince Emma to forget her scheme to pair her up with Jakob. "You know when I told you I didn't want to upset Jakob? Here's a way to look at it from his point of view. How would you feel if you were forced to sit beside Kyle through dinner?"

Emma sat thoughtful for a minute and then said, "*Jah*, I see what you mean. I don't think Sam has mentioned it to Jakob yet. I'll tell him we've changed our minds."

Sarah had never changed hers, but she wasn't about to quibble with her sister. She was just relieved that Emma finally understood.

Her sister tapped her fingers on the arm of the couch. "But who will we pair you with?"

"No one." Sarah sat alone at other weddings or slipped off before the meal so her friends didn't feel obligated to match her up. She most enjoyed being seated with her friends' out-of-town relatives. She could engage in a friendly conversation with them, knowing she'd most likely never see them again.

The twist of Emma's lips made it clear her sister would never let her sit alone.

Sarah sighed inwardly. If she sat without a partner, she could watch Jakob without having to worry about carrying on a slow-moving, awkward conversation, but her sister seemed determined to pair her up. "I have an idea," Sarah said. "Why don't you seat me with one of Sam's cousins from Big Valley?"

Emma frowned. "Long-distance courtships can be difficult."

"I'm not interested in dating anyone."

"Do you remember earlier when I said it would do Kyle good to let go of the past and find someone else? Maybe you should do that too."

Sarah only shook her head. Although her sister's words made sense, her heart refused to cooperate.

"Emma," someone shouted. "The wedding trailer is here."

Her sister jumped up from the couch. "Oh, no, will people be able to tell I've been crying?"

Sarah stood and pinched Emma's cheeks. "There now, your cheeks are rosy." That would make the redness rimming Emma's eyes less noticeable.

"*Danke*, Sarah, for everything." Emma's lips curved into a smile, and her eyes sparkled. "I can hardly believe tomorrow I'll marry Sam." She practically danced out of the room. Emma had always been the emotional one, clouds and storm one minute, sunshine the next. Her parents had tried to suppress her moods, to get her to act calmly and sedately. Thankfully, Sam enjoyed Emma's liveliness.

Sarah stayed for a moment to erase images of Jakob from her mind. Setting the tables with wedding china would keep her hands occupied, but it would be hard to keep her thoughts from straying to daydreams.

When she reached the front door, the men were unloading chairs and benches, and several women had left the kitchen to help shuttle dishes. Sarah joined them. When she returned for another load, a buggy pulled into the driveway. The minute it stopped, Rebecca hopped out and raced across the lawn toward Sarah, a wicker carrier over each arm.

Sarah's heart lifted as it always did when she saw

her best friend. The two of them had become insepa-
rable since Sarah began working as Rebecca's teaching assistant at the schoolhouse. Rebecca had kindly
offered to teach alone so Sarah could help with wedding preparations.

Sarah's pulse tripped faster when Jakob rounded the
buggy to help his mother, who carried two baskets.
Then he hefted a large box and headed toward the front
porch, his face set in determined lines.

Although Sarah tried to keep her attention on Rebecca's chatter, all she wanted to do was follow Jakob's
progress across the yard. She interrupted her friend
midsentence. "Oh, let me run and hold the door open
for Jakob and your mother. That box looks heavy, and
your *mamm* has her arms full."

"I do too," Rebecca pouted.

"Let me help you." Sarah snatched one of the wicker
carriers Rebecca was holding and dashed to the porch,
arriving breathless as Jakob mounted the first step. He
slipped past her, setting her heart pounding even harder
when her sleeve brushed his arm.

"I'll take this to the kitchen, shall I?" Jakob said.
"*Mamm* insisted on bringing roasters and extra pots."

"That's wonderful. We can use more." Sarah's words
came out overly enthusiastic. Had she given away her
feelings? She forced herself to turn to Mary Zook. "It
was wonderful *gut* of you to bring them."

Jakob's mother smiled at her. "*Jah*, I remember your
mamm needed more when Lydia got married."

Sarah sucked in a breath and glanced at Jakob. He
had his back to her, but he'd stiffened when his mother
said Lydia's name. To ease the tension, she said, "You
remember where the kitchen is," and then wished she

could bite her tongue. Of course, he remembered the way to the kitchen. He'd gone there all the time when he was courting Lydia.

Mary Zook laughed. "We do for sure and certain. Haven't we been here many times already? I'm guessing all the wedding preparations have made you a bit *ferhoodled.*"

"That's true." Sarah only hoped no one realized the real reason.

Rebecca patted her arm as she passed. "I expect you're exhausted. Weddings are so much work." She sighed. "But they're so exciting, aren't they?"

As soon as Rebecca was inside, Sarah closed the door behind her and hurried down the hall after her friend, hoping to get a glimpse of Jakob. He likely wouldn't talk to her, but being in the same room would be heavenly.

She was wrong.

Jakob turned as she came through the kitchen door and gave her a friendly smile. "Where should I put this box?"

"Oh." She was so flustered she couldn't answer. She wanted to keep staring at his black bangs, his deep brown eyes, the curve of his lips... She tore her gaze away, her face hot. "The table." She pointed to the kitchen table and realized every space was covered with pies, cakes, and serving dishes. "I, umm, wait, let me pull out the bench a bit."

She dragged the bench out and then stepped back so he could set the box down, drinking in his strong arms from all the woodworking, his broad back as he straightened up.

"Danke," she whispered, her voice dreamy.

He blinked at her. "You're welcome."

Mary Zook came up behind her, startling her. "Shall I set these baskets on the bench too?"

Sarah broke eye contact with Jakob and turned her attention to his mother. "Yes, please." She motioned for Rebecca to set her carrier down too. "We're grateful for all this."

"And we're happy to help." Mary Zook nodded to Jakob. "You'd better head home. Why don't you come back for us just before dark?"

Sarah's heart sank. Jakob wouldn't be staying.

"We had an early supper, but Jakob needs to stay with his *dat*," Mary explained. "Hiriam hasn't been doing well the past few days."

"Oh, I'm sorry to hear that." Sarah longed to stare at Jakob as he walked down the hall, but she stayed facing his mother.

"We weren't sure Jakob could attend the wedding, but one of Hiriam's cousins will come out to stay with him tomorrow."

Bishop Zook had suffered a stroke a short while after Emma's accident four years ago. Then he'd had another six months ago and never fully recovered. As the only son, Jakob had taken over his *dat*'s woodworking business, but he also spent a lot of time at home, helping to care for his father.

Rebecca came over and grabbed Sarah's arm. "Have they set up the tables downstairs?" When Sarah nodded, she pulled her toward the stairway. "Let's go help with the dishes. I can't wait to see how everything looks."

With one quick glance over her shoulder to be sure Jakob wasn't still lingering in the hallway, Sarah allowed herself to be dragged to the basement, where sun streamed through the small windows high on the walls, making the glassware sparkle.

"Oh, isn't everything beautiful!" Rebecca enthused over the ribbon-festooned vases of celery, the fruit centerpieces, and the wedding cake on the *eck*.

As part of the bridal party, Sarah and Sam's sister would sit beside Emma at this corner table. Two of Sam's brothers would flank the groom for the meal.

Sarah took a moment to appreciate the beauty, but then set to work laying out plates and silverware. With two hundred guests expected tomorrow, they'd have to have two seatings for the meals. She hoped staying busy would keep her thoughts on the wedding, but pictures of Jakob flashed through her mind. The deep timbre of his voice as he'd asked where to set the box. His cheeks ruddy from the cold. The strength of his arms as he'd lifted the box.

Rebecca nudged her. "Are you all right? You've been standing there holding the same plate for a while now."

Sarah started. She'd let her imagination run away with her. "I'm sorry," she said, hoping Rebecca hadn't guessed the subject of her daydreams. She and her friend shared everything with each other, but Sarah had never confided about her crush on Rebecca's brother.

"Were you dreaming about your own wedding?" Rebecca giggled. "I know I am. I can't wait."

"Abner asked you?" Neither he nor Rebecca had been baptized yet, so it was much too early for them to be thinking about courting, let alone marriage.

"Not yet, but he will."

Sarah sighed. It must be lovely to have that much confidence in someone's love. Her thoughts were so far away, she almost missed Rebecca's whisper.

"Speaking of Abner, I have to talk to you *alone*. Not now when everything's so busy, but once the wedding's over?"

"Of course."

What had etched those frown lines between Rebecca's brows and thinned her lips into a tight line? Was she having problems in her relationship? She'd seemed so sure of Abner's marriage proposal a few minutes ago.

"Are you and Abner having trouble?" She kept her voice low so no one around them could hear.

"Abner and me? No, not at all." Rebecca glanced away as she said it, but not before Sarah caught a glimpse of uncertainty in her eyes. "This is about Jakob."

Sarah's breathing constricted. "Jakob?"

"*Jah*, Jakob." A grim expression on her face, she waved a hand and mumbled something about "problems, big problems."

Gripping her friend's arm, Sarah said, "We can go somewhere now and talk."

Rebecca shook her head. "It can wait. Besides it'll take too long to explain." Shaking off Sarah's hand, Rebecca went for more plates, leaving Sarah staring after her, worry curdling her stomach.

Jakob? What could be wrong with Jakob that could cause such deep lines on Rebecca's face? How could she possibly wait until after the wedding to find out?

But Sarah had no chance to talk to Rebecca alone before Jakob arrived to pick them up. Sarah peeked out the window as he helped his mother into the buggy, telling herself she was checking to be sure he was all right. But the moonlight shining down revealed nothing, except that Jakob appeared as ruggedly handsome in semi-darkness as he did in the daylight.

Chapter Eight

Everyone rose before dawn the next morning. *Dat* and the boys had done the milking while Sarah prepared breakfast for the family and guests. They had barely finished when women from church arrived. Laughing and chattering, they filled warming pans with mashed potatoes, chicken mixed with filling, and creamed celery. Sarah took advantage of the commotion to slip away with a tray for the *daadi haus*.

As usual, the two men were asleep. She set the tray down, debating over whether or not to wake them. The meal would taste better warm, and there'd be no time to reheat it later. She had to hurry and get ready.

Just then *Mammi* came downstairs dressed for the wedding. She took one look at the tray and clapped her hands, startling both men. "Time to get up and eat," she commanded. "We have a busy day ahead of us."

Herman's sleep-dulled eyes sharpened into alertness. "Today's the wedding, isn't it?"

"Exactly," *Mammi* said, "which is why you need to eat quickly. Sarah has a lot to do today. She can't be waiting around while you two lollygag."

Paul stretched and yawned, then grabbed a plate and fork from the tray and handed it to Herman before he took his own. He shoveled the food in and swilled down the coffee. "That was tasty."

Herman picked at the food. "What time does the shindig begin?"

"Eight."

"Isn't that rather late? Don't you people usually go to bed early?"

"I don't think she means tonight, dude," Paul said. "Didn't you hear all those horses clip-clopping up the driveway this morning?"

"Those were some of the church ladies," Sarah said. "They arrived around six or so with the food."

Herman's jaw dropped. "You must pay pretty good to get them out here that early. Why don't you hold the wedding at a decent hour?"

"We don't pay anyone to help with the cooking. They're all volunteers. We all help each other."

"Whoa, you gotta be kidding. People actually get up at dawn and cook for free?"

"That's right," *Mammi* said. "Now eat that breakfast. No time to waste."

The tartness of her tone made Herman pick up a small morsel on his fork. He examined it and then turned up his nose. "What's this?"

"Scrapple."

"Huh? What's scrapple?" He looked like a sulky child.

"I don't think you want to know," Paul said. "Just like it's best not to know what's in hot dogs. Scrapple tastes good, though, so just eat it."

Herman had just put the bite in his mouth when *Mammi* said, "It's made from hog offal."

He choked and spit it out on his plate. "Offal? What the, um, *heck* is that?"

"The head and innards, like the liver and heart, mixed with cornmeal, some flour, and spices."

"Gross."

Mammi snatched his plate and handed it to Paul. "I suggest you eat this. We probably won't be able to get back here until late afternoon with any more food."

"What about me?" Herman squawked.

"Good thing you don't like to eat." *Mammi* took Sarah's arm. "We'd better hurry. It wouldn't do to be late for your sister's wedding."

"But, *Mammi*, we can't let him go hungry."

"Let's leave that decision up to Paul."

"Wait a minute," Herman said. "Those ladies you mentioned. They're all working in the kitchen now?" He had a cagey look on his face.

"Yes, but we won't be eating for hours." *Mammi* shook a finger at him. "And you're not to go disturbing them, begging for anything."

"I had no intention of doing that."

"Oh, that's right," *Mammi* retorted. "I forgot. You can't get out of bed with that broken leg of yours."

Sarah glanced at *Mammi* curiously. She sounded almost as if she didn't believe his leg was hurt. That reminded her of Kyle's comment about the walking cast.

A flash of something flickered in Herman's eyes. Fear?

She waited until they were outside to ask *Mammi* about her suspicions.

"Tell me something, Sarah." *Mammi* stopped walking and turned toward her. "What do people with broken legs usually do? They get around on crutches, right? So why does Herman insist he can't get out of bed?"

"I don't know, but the doctor did say he had bad breaks and shouldn't be moved. Maybe Herman's worried his leg won't heal properly."

"All right. Then explain this. How does Herman manage to go to the bathroom?"

Sarah had so many other things on her mind that it hadn't occurred to her to wonder about things like that. "I guess that's why Paul's around to help."

"Do you think Paul carries him?"

"No, I imagine he helps him walk... Oh." Sarah couldn't believe she'd been so focused on the wedding and Jakob, she neglected to put simple clues together. Mary Zook was right when she'd called her *ferhoodled*. "Oh, and *Mammi*, Kyle said it's a walking cast, so Herman can get around easily."

Mammi nodded. "Ah, that explains it. Twice I thought he seemed to be scrambling back into bed when I was coming downstairs. I wasn't quite sure, though."

Now that *Mammi* had voiced her suspicions, Sarah's mind started whirling. What did the two men want? Why were they here? Who were they hiding from?

But when she posed those questions, *Mammi* only shrugged. "That's really not my business. I think God brought them here for a reason, and we need to trust Him to show us His purpose."

Mammi was right, but Sarah wanted answers to her questions. Maybe after the wedding, they could find out. For now, she needed to concentrate on Emma and Sam, but she did have one thing she wanted to do first.

When she and *Mammi* reached the kitchen, Sarah checked the time. She had half an hour before she needed to get dressed. She should help in the kitchen, but she felt sorry for Herman. Yes, he was disagreeable and possibly untrustworthy, but that didn't mean he should go hungry. And it bothered Sarah that he and Paul would have to wait until later in the afternoon to eat. She took six of the cinnamon buns Herman had liked, some fruit, several slices of bread, and some church spread and hurried back to the *daadi haus*. When she opened the door, sounds of an argument reached her ears.

"If they get upset, they'll tell everyone," Paul said. "Then no one will cooperate with you. You don't understand how they operate. They all stick together."

"Just do what I say. This is a golden opportunity right under our noses. We'd be foolish to waste it."

"I don't think it's right."

"If you won't do it, I'll do it myself," Herman said in a tight, angry voice.

"Have at it," Paul replied. "But I'm not taking another chance of getting caught."

"We pulled that one off, didn't we?"

"I'm not so sure."

Sarah felt guilty about eavesdropping, but she didn't know how to let them know she was there. At the same time, she wondered if their conversation might give her some clues as to what they were doing or who they were hiding from. But her conscience wouldn't let her keep listening.

"I've brought more food," she called out.

Strange scrambling noises ensued. By the time she reached the doorway, Herman was frantically tossing the blanket over his legs, but not before she caught a glimpse of gray plastic along the side of his leg and black straps running across it. Several years ago *Dat* had his leg strapped up exactly like that for a badly twisted ankle, and he'd managed to do the milking and all the chores with it on. So Kyle and *Mammi* were right about Herman being able to get around. She suspected if she'd arrived at the living room entrance a little sooner, she'd have seen him standing.

"What are you doing back here?" Herman griped. "I thought you had a wedding to attend."

Sarah set down the food. "I didn't want you to go hungry. I know you liked the cinnamon buns yesterday, so I brought you some of those. I also have some sandwich fixings for your lunch." She handed Herman a plate with three cinnamon rolls on it.

"You didn't have to do that," he said gruffly, but she could tell by his expression that he was surprised and touched.

Maybe God was softening his heart. Sarah prayed for both men as she hurried back to the house to dress.

When she entered the bedroom, Emma was alone. Sam's sisters must have already dressed. Her sister was pacing around the room, her blue skirt and white apron swishing. "I wish Leah wasn't coming." Her black high-topped shoes made little stamping sounds as she moved.

"Leah? Who's Leah?"

"Sam's old girlfriend. The one who broke his heart by marrying his cousin."

"But if she's married…?"

"Still, Sam might see her, remember how much he loved her. What if he changes his mind about marrying me? What if he decides he made a mistake and leaves?" Her face pinched, she hurried to the window as if expecting to see Sam galloping off in his buggy.

"Calm down." Sarah crossed the room and patted her sister's hand, which was gripping the windowsill. "Sam loves you and has no intention of leaving."

Emma turned toward her, but fearfulness remained in her eyes. "Maybe he'll realize…"

Sarah knew Emma was worried about her past, and she hastened to finish her sister's sentence. "…you love him and will make him a wonderful wife."

"But Leah?"

"If Sam loved her, he'd never have asked you to marry him. He's not that kind of person."

"You're right. He's the most honorable person I know."

Sarah could think of another man, one she thought of as even more honorable, but she reassured her sister, "You can count on Sam. Besides, you saw Kyle yesterday." She hated to remind Emma of this, but it might help her sister put things in perspective. "Did that make you change your mind about Sam?"

"No," Emma shouted, then she quieted. "A thousand times no. It only made me appreciate Sam more and made me realize how right he is for me. It increased the love I feel for him."

"So," Sarah said quietly, "don't you think seeing Leah might do the same for Sam? Make him realize how glad he is to have you?"

Emma sniffled. "Do you really think so?"

Sarah patted her sister's back. "I know so."

"But what if he changes his mind and doesn't show up." Emma paced over to the bed and sat down.

"He's already here, and his whole family is here, so I'm sure he's planning to marry you. Why don't you go down and ask him?"

"No, I don't want to put ideas in his head. Or let him know I doubted his love."

"Right," Sarah said. "Wait to tell him until after he's gone through with it. Then he'll already be stuck with you."

Emma gasped. Then she studied Sarah's face and giggled. "You're teasing me, aren't you?"

"No, I'm serious. At least the part about Sam loving you. Anyone who looks at him can see his feelings shining in his eyes."

A brilliant smile on her face, Emma sat, clasping her pillow as if she were hugging Sam. "Oh, Sarah, you're right. You always know how to make people feel better." She dropped the pillow, threw her arms around Sarah, and hugged her.

"I love you, Em." After one final squeeze, Sarah disentangled herself from her sister's embrace to begin dressing. "I know this day is going to be special."

"Thanks, Sarah. I'm so glad you're going to be in my bridal party." Emma nibbled on her lower lip. "I forgot to tell you. I hope you won't be too upset with me."

"Of course not, Em," Sarah assured her. "What is it?"

"Sam talked to Jakob."

Sarah's hand slipped, and she poked herself in the side with the straight pin she was using to fasten her dress.

"And Jakob said yes."

He said YES!!! Blood pounded in Sarah's head and ears, making her dizzy. She forced herself to draw in a breath. She'd sit with him at the meal tonight and— And he'd be miserable. Poor Jakob.

"Oh, Emma, I'm sure he only said yes to be polite."

"Maybe not. Maybe he said yes because he enjoys

your company. You can talk about growing up, times you shared. Maybe he'll remember all the good times you had together and see you as someone he'd like to date."

If only… "I doubt it." Sarah felt guilty making such a fuss about sitting with Jakob and causing Emma distress on her wedding day. "I'm sorry, I didn't mean to make you feel bad. You're probably right, we can talk about childhood, share memories."

"I hope it works out." Emma swallowed hard. "We need to go downstairs now. It's almost time."

Sarah hastily pinned the rest of the dress, pricking herself as she went along. *Mamm* still insisted her daughters use pins to close their dresses. Sarah had never objected to it before, but today of all days, she wished for hooks and eyes. Her fingers were clumsy, and the pins were crooked.

"Are you ready?" Emma asked, then held out her trembling hands. "I've never been so nervous in my life. Look at how I'm shaking, and my throat is so dry, I can scarcely swallow."

Sarah was experiencing the same symptoms. Just the thought of seeing Jakob dressed in his black jacket, spending time with him, trying to talk to him without giving away her feelings, had her quivering inside. But she pushed aside her own panic. This was Emma's wedding day. She needed to concentrate on her sister's feelings. "Why don't I go downstairs and get you a drink of water?"

"No, let's just go down together. I should have been down there helping, but I'm trembling so much, I'm worried I'll spill or drop something."

"*Mamm* has plenty of help." Sarah motioned for Emma to precede her out the door.

At the sight of her sister's black prayer covering, a symbol that she would become a married woman today, tears sprang to Sarah's eyes. Although she reminded herself she wasn't losing a sister, she was gaining a wonderful brother-in-law, their childhood together had come to an end. Never again would Emma sleep in the bed next to her, giggle with her at night, or confide secrets in the dark.

After today, of these three beds their grandfather had lovingly carved and the three matching Lone Star quilts *Mamm* had painstakingly sewed, only one bed and quilt would remain in use. This room had once held three sisters; now it would hold only one. With misty eyes, Sarah closed the bedroom door behind her.

Chapter Nine

Guests were already pulling up outside by the time Sarah and Emma reached the kitchen. One of the women shooed them out to the living room, where the sliding panel between her parents' room and the living room had been opened. Benches had been lined up in the living room for the men, and now several men were setting up benches on the women's side of the room.

"I never thought I'd see this day," Emma whispered. Then she caught sight of Sam, carrying in another bench. "He's here."

At the relief in her sister's voice, Sarah nudged her. "Of course, he is. Why wouldn't he be?"

"I don't know. I just worried…" Emma's words trailed off as Sam caught sight of her and nearly dropped the bench in his hands.

He tore his gaze away and stared at the bench as if he couldn't remember why he was holding it. Then he shook himself, set it in place, and met Emma's eyes again.

Sarah hoped she didn't look that besotted when she watched Jakob. If she was honest, though, she often

dreamed of Jakob looking at her the way Sam was staring at Emma. Sarah pushed the image aside. Today was
her sister's wedding day. She wouldn't think about—
or worry about—Jakob until later, when she had to sit
with him at the meal. Although she was dreading it for
his sake, her heart sang.

Outside, several vans pulled up, dropping off more
guests. Sarah hurried to the door to invite them in,
greeting the ones from her *g'may* and introducing herself to the ones from Sam's. When Leah Stoltzfus gave
her name and that of her husband, Sarah didn't regis-
ter his name because she was too busy studying Sam's
ex-girlfriend.

Just then Sam crossed the hall, and Leah called out
his name. He approached, shook both their hands with
a polite smile, and thanked them for coming, but he
immediately turned his attention to an older couple on
the porch. He hurried over to help the woman over the
doorsill and, with a genuine smile, introduced them to
Sarah. Although four married couples were serving as
forgeher to seat the guests, Sam personally escorted
the older couple into the room. Then he and Emma
passed through the hallway with the bishop, going off
for their private talk.

Sarah had been so caught up watching Sam's reaction
to Leah, so she could report to Emma that Sam had absolutely no interest in his former girlfriend, she'd forgotten to close the front door. A blast of cold air blew into
the hallway, and she shivered. Before she could shut the
door, another van parked, and a group of *Englischers*
piled out with large bags slung over their shoulders.
They weren't coming to the wedding, were they?

They headed for the front door, so evidently, they

were. They must be Sam's friends. Maybe they worked with him. Sarah was surprised they'd come for the service instead of the dinner, but she opened the door and shook their hands. The three men and one woman scanned the hallway.

"Which way to the wedding?" the tall red-haired man asked.

One of the married couples came over and offered to escort them in, but when the wife tried to take the lady to the woman's benches, she resisted.

"We all stay together," she insisted.

The men ignored the usher's attempt to seat them. "We'll stand back here."

As Sarah passed them to take her seat, the redheaded man, who seemed to be the group leader, asked loudly, "Where are the bride and groom?"

The usher responded in a hushed voice, "The bishop is counseling them, but the service is about to begin." Again, he tried to seat them, but the men refused.

At eight a.m., the congregation broke into song. A clattering of metal drowned out the notes of the first hymn. People swiveled in their seats to see the group setting up tripods and camera equipment.

Mammi rushed toward them. "What do you think you're doing?"

"Filming the wedding. What does it look like?" the redhead answered flippantly.

"Mind your manners, young man," *Mammi* warned. "Take those cameras out of here. You have no right to film this."

Dat reached the back of the room. "We don't allow films or cameras. You're welcome to stay if you put them away. Are you friends of Sam's?"

"Sam who?" one of the men asked.

"The groom," *Mammi* snapped. "If you don't know Sam, why are you here?"

"We have a contract to film this wedding."

"You most certainly don't." *Mammi* set her hands on her hips. "We'd never authorize such a thing. It's against our beliefs."

While the redhead rifled through the outer pocket of his bag and pulled out a sheaf of papers, the woman walked down the center aisle, flicked on her video camera, and panned the room. Jakob rushed over and placed himself in front of the camera, shielding Sarah and the other attendants.

"Get out of the way," the woman yelped. "You're ruining the picture."

Wherever she moved the camera, Jakob stood between her and people she was trying to film so all she got were pictures of his chest. With a huff, she turned off her camera.

"This is a bust," she said. "We'd better get paid well for coming all this way for nothing."

Jakob followed her down the aisle. When they reached the back of the room, he picked up her camera bag and tripod. "I'll help you carry these out."

She gave him a dirty look but set her video camera in the bag he held out. After she fastened the bag, she snatched it from his hand. "No one touches my equipment," she snarled.

Jakob's expression remained unruffled. "Fine. Let me show you to the door."

Before he could accompany her, she stalked to the hallway. A few seconds later, the door banged.

Dat turned to the men. "If you aren't here to take

part in the wedding, I'm afraid you'll have to go too," he said. "I won't have my daughter's wedding disrupted like this."

"What do you plan to do about it? You can't make us leave, and I've been assured the Amish don't sue or call the cops, so you can't hurt us legally." The redhead flashed *Dat* a cruel smile.

"We do depend on the *police* when necessary, young man," *Mammi* snapped. "And it seems it might be an appropriate time because you're trespassing on private property."

"Go ahead and call them," the redhead challenged her. "They'll arrive and see we have a signed request for filming." He unfolded the papers in his hand and stuck them under *Dat*'s nose.

Dat glanced over the first page. "I see a request to film at our address, but none of us agreed to it."

"It's just your usual standard contract with all the legalese." The man flipped through the pages until he got to the end. "But it's been signed right here." He smoothed out the paper and poked his finger at the bottom of the page. "Right there."

In a shaky voice, *Dat* read aloud, "Signed this day by..." He gasped. "Sarah Esh."

Every eye in the room turned toward her.

Chapter Ten

Sarah's mind whirled. She'd never have signed any contract like that. Surely *Dat* knew that. Yet everyone stared at her accusingly. Her throat was so tight with unshed tears, she couldn't respond. They couldn't believe she'd do something like this to ruin her sister's wedding.

Then a deep voice rang out from the back of the room. "Sarah Esh would never have signed that contract. Or any contract for that matter."

Jakob. He was defending her. He believed in her.

Dat blinked, then repeated Jakob's words. "My daughter would not have signed any such document. Did you, Sarah?" His voice shook as if he were a bit uncertain of the validity of his words.

Jakob had believed in her when her own father was unsure.

But *Dat* was beckoning her. "Come here, *dochder*, and look at this signature."

Her face burning, Sarah stood and, with all eyes on her, walked down the aisle to where the redhead was brandishing the document. She held her head high, afraid if she bowed it, people might assume she was hiding her guilt. The distance from her bench to the back of the room seemed to stretch for miles.

Jakob's gaze and understanding smile kept her moving forward when she wanted to run and hide. When she reached the back, *Dat* took the paper and jabbed his thumb at the signature line. "That your signature, Sarah?"

Of course, it wasn't her signature. Sarah didn't have to look at it to know, but she pretended to examine it carefully, though the words blurred before her eyes. She shook her head.

Jakob squinted at the contract. "I've seen Sarah's writing. It's small, delicate, and precise. That scrawl looks more like a man's signature." He tilted his head to one side and asked in a polite tone, "It wouldn't be yours, would it?"

"Are you calling me a liar?" Fists clenched at his sides, the redhead drew himself up to his full height and stared down his nose at Jakob.

"I would never think of calling another person a liar."

The man blinked as if struggling to make sense of Jakob's comments. "This paper was emailed to me. I didn't sign anything. Maybe another Sarah Esh signed it."

"I suppose that's possible," *Dat* said. "But there aren't any other Sarah Eshes in this community and certainly not at this address."

Jakob moved toward one of the other men, who was standing nearby, watching the discussion. "I'd be happy to help you carry your things out to the van."

"I don't need help." He looked to the redhead as if for direction.

The redhead shrugged. "If it's a forged document,

we'd better scram. No point in getting questioned by the cops."

The three of them stowed their equipment, slung the bags over their shoulders, and walked into the hallway. *Dat* trailed them into the hallway, and when the front door opened and shut, a collective exhale sounded in the room.

After giving Jakob a grateful glance, Sarah walked back up the aisle to murmurings of "what a shame" and "sorry it happened." She sank into place, and the singing resumed. For a while Sarah only mouthed the words. Her pulse still raced so fast she could barely catch her breath. She tried to tell herself it was from the confrontation that had just occurred, but if she were completely honest, having Jakob stand so close to her and hearing him defend her had played a part in her rapidly beating heart.

When she could breathe normally, the joy in her soul overflowed in song. Nearby Lydia sat cradling baby Elizabeth in her arms, beaming across the room at Caleb, who had baby Aaron's head resting on his shoulder. The love in his eyes as he gazed at his wife and daughter added to Sarah's happiness. Both her sisters had chosen good men.

Her gladness increased when Emma and Sam entered. With his slightly crooked smile, Sam appeared nervous, but he gazed down at Emma with adoration. Emma looked as if she were holding back tears. A lump in her throat, Sarah watched them take their places for the sermons.

Each part of the service was bittersweet for Sarah as she knelt for prayer and listened to the Scripture reading and sermons. The reminders of God's design for marriage and stories of biblical marriages through the ages touched her heart because today her sister would become part of that age-old tradition. Her eyes filled with tears as the minister asked Sam and Emma to step forward with the congregation. With bowed heads and solemn faces, they stood before him. While the congregation surrounded and supported them, the final part of the wedding service began.

The familiar questions took on special meaning for Sarah because Emma was taking these vows with her beloved Sam. First the bishop asked Sam and Emma: "Can you both confess and believe that God has ordained marriage to be a union between one man and one wife, and do you also have the confidence that you are approaching marriage in accordance with the way you have been taught?"

Sarah's lips trembled when Sam's hearty *yes* blended with Emma's softer one.

Then he turned to Sam. "Do you also have confidence, brother, that the Lord has provided this, our sister, as a marriage partner for you?"

Any doubts or worries Emma had expressed earlier would be erased by Sam's rapid and definite *yes*. He made it clear that Emma was the only woman for him. Sam's dedication to her sister made Sarah love her brother-in-law even more than she already did.

She tried to close her mind to the pictures flooding her imagination—of Jakob standing before the bishop to take the same vows. Of herself in Emma's place, answering those questions with surety and love. But she pushed those daydreams away because if Jakob ever took those vows, it would be with someone else. That would hurt too much to bear.

She'd been so deep in thought, she almost missed Emma's answer to the question, "Do you also have the confidence, sister, that the Lord has provided this, our brother, as a marriage partner for you?"

Her sister's voice wavered slightly, but Sarah could detect the deep love behind Emma's *yes*. Remembering her sister's trembling hands earlier, Sarah said a quick prayer that God would calm Emma's nerves.

Then the bishop asked Sam, "Do you also promise your wife that if she should in bodily weakness, sickness, or any similar circumstances need your help, that you will care for her as is fitting for a Christian husband?" And again, his *yes* was unhesitating and strong. And Emma's *yes* to the matching question sounded clearer and firmer. Sarah had no doubt Emma would willingly care for Sam as a Christian wife should. If only Sarah's own lot in life could include such a promise.

She leaned forward eagerly to hear the final question. "Do you both promise together that you will with love, forbearance, and patience live with each other, and not part from each other until God will separate you in death?"

Both Emma and Sam affirmed that with an emphatic *yes*.

The prayer that followed left Sarah so teary-eyed she could barely see the bishop take Emma's hand and place it in Sam's, but the closing words rang in her ears. "The God of Abraham and the God of Isaac, and the God of Jacob be with you and help you together and give His blessings richly unto you, and this through Jesus Christ." Sarah mouthed the *amen* at the end with the bishop, rejoicing in the clasped hands that symbolized Sam and Emma's union.

The beauty of the service stayed with Sarah as everyone filed out for the first meal. She was grateful to sit on the girls' side of the table to the left of Emma and Sam. Sam's sister sat beside her, and they chatted as they ate their chicken filling casserole, mashed potatoes, gravy, creamed celery, peppered cabbage, and applesauce. Despite the lively conversation, Sarah's thoughts and gaze kept returning to Jakob, who sat on the opposite side of the room for this first meal. She tried to confine herself to surreptitious peeks, but it was difficult not to admire him in his crisp white shirt and black jacket. She searched his face for signs of how painful the wedding had been for him. Emma looked so much like Lydia, he must have seen the comparison. And how difficult it must have been for him to watch Lydia and Caleb exchange loving glances as they held the twins.

At least he was spared the sight of them at the meal. Lydia had slipped upstairs to feed the babies and put them down for their naps, and Caleb had joined her, bringing plates of food for both of them.

Sarah had a hard time choosing between cream-filled doughnuts, cherry pie, and tapioca pudding for dessert, so she had some of each. She'd just put a bite of pie in her mouth when Sam's sister Annie poked her.

"Is that your boyfriend?" Annie waved a hand to indicate Jakob.

"What? No, no, he's not." Had she made her interest in him so obvious that even strangers guessed? And had Jakob noticed her staring at him?

To her relief, he seemed engrossed in a conversation with one of Sam's relatives seated beside him.

Annie's mouth turned down. "Oh, I thought with the way you were studying him…"

"I'm worried about him. He was Lydia's boyfriend—" she still got a pang when she said those words "—but she married Caleb. Poor Jakob was heartbroken."

"Oh, that's so sad. He's quite handsome."

Jealousy flickered through Sarah, but she responded, "Yes, he is."

"So you think he hasn't gotten over your sister?"

"I'm pretty sure he hasn't." Why was Annie asking all these questions? Was she interested? Maybe she'd hint to Sam that she'd like to be paired with Jakob for the evening meal. Sarah almost asked Annie if she'd like to do that, but it would hurt too much to see him with anyone else.

During the hymn sing that followed the meal, Sarah slipped out and offered to help the women in the kitchen who were washing the dishes. She worked in silence, listening with only one ear to the chatter and gossip around her. Her nervousness about possibly sitting with Jakob grew stronger with each revolution of the clock hands. What if she ended up so tongue-tied she couldn't speak to him and they sat silent throughout meal?

When the women weren't looking, Sarah sneaked several servings of the chicken filling casserole from the warmer onto a piece of foil. She tucked them into Rebecca's empty wicker carrier along with some red beet eggs and slices of pie. That would have to do for Paul and Herman until after the evening meal.

While everyone was engrossed in their tasks, she slipped out the door. This time she banged open the door of the *daadi haus* to warn them she was there.

When she reached the living room, Herman was in bed with his legs covered, yet they both had guilty looks on their faces.

Paul sniffed the air as she unwrapped the casserole. "That smells delicious."

When she handed Herman his portion, he dove right in. "At last! Something recognizable," he said. But a short while later, he poked at the red beet egg. "What's this? A leftover Easter egg? It feels rubbery."

Paul laughed. "Haven't you ever had Harvard beets? Those eggs are made with pickled beet juice."

Herman continued to glare at the egg. "How do you know so much about the Amish?"

"I read up on them when you told me your idea to—" Paul snapped his mouth shut.

His idea to what? Hoping they'd continue their conversation, Sarah turned her back and busied herself with unwrapping the pie. But as if they'd made a pact of silence, neither one said a word.

Paul, as usual, expressed his thanks for the food and tucked into the pie. "So where's your sister going on her honeymoon?"

"Honeymoon?" Sarah gave him a blank look.

"You know, where are they going tonight? Are they taking a trip anywhere special?"

"They'll stay here tonight, so they can help clean up the house tomorrow."

Herman snorted. "Well, doesn't that sound like a fun way to spend the first day of marriage?"

"Oh, right." Paul mumbled. "I remember reading that. Everyone does it, don't they?"

"Of course." Sarah handed each of them a piece of cherry pie.

For once, Herman didn't complain. He dug in eagerly. "So they don't go anywhere?" He directed his question to Paul, but Sarah answered.

"They'll leave on Friday for Big Valley where they'll stay with a different one of Sam's relatives for each meal during the weekend."

"That's when they get their wedding gifts, isn't it?" When she nodded, Paul beamed, looking as thrilled as her students when they won a spelling bee.

"What's that noise?" Herman asked.

Sarah stopped and listened. A distant melody from the *Ausbund* lilted through the air. "Do you mean the hymn sing?"

"That's singing? It sounds more like yodeling or chanting."

Whatever it sounded like to Herman, she needed to get back before she was missed. "I'd better get going." She collected the wicker carrier and headed to the house. Time was passing quickly. It would soon be time for the boys to head out to the barn.

She made it to the kitchen as a group of girls surged up the steps to her bedroom to prepare for the afternoon snack.

"There you are!" Rebecca detached herself from the group to link arms with Sarah. "Come on," she said, giving Sarah's arm a tug. "Let's go upstairs."

Reluctantly, Sarah joined the mass of chattering girls. Instead of feeling their party-like excitement, her spirits dipped. The boys would arrive soon to claim a girl for the snack. Would Jakob feel obligated to pair up with her for this, or had he changed his mind?

Rebecca nattered nonstop about Abner, for which Sarah was grateful. It kept her mind off the upcoming meal. Other girls joined the conversation from time to time, but many of them flitted off to Zeke and Abe's bedroom at the back of the house, where they'd have a view of the barn and possibly a glimpse of their boyfriends.

As it neared three o'clock, Rebecca clutched Sarah's arm and dragged her into her brothers' room, so they could peek out at the barn. Rebecca slipped past some of the other girls who were crowded at the window and pulled Sarah with her. "How long do you think it will take for them to come for us?"

"I don't know." If Sarah had her way, it would be forever. She wished the men and boys would stay out in the barn and skip the snack.

Other girls elbowed them away from the window.

"Why so glum?" Rebecca teased, then sobered. "I'm sorry, Sarah. You're so pretty and sweet, I don't understand why all the boys aren't flocking around you." She nibbled on her lower lip for a moment before saying, "Maybe someone nice will ask to accompany you."

Oh, *jah*, someone nice had agreed to sit with her. Someone spectacular, in fact. Someone Sarah was too nervous to talk to.

"Isn't there anyone you'd really like to date?"

The sympathy in Rebecca's voice made Sarah squirm. The two of them confided all their secrets to each other, but how could she tell her best friend the truth?

One of the girls by the window squealed, "They're coming."

Sarah's stomach churned, but she wasn't sure if it was in anticipation or fear.

Chapter Eleven

The press of girls around the window dissolved as they rushed downstairs to greet their boyfriends or to stand outside waiting for someone to ask them to pair up. After the first gaggle of girls left, Sarah stepped out of the way, so other boys could find their dates. As more couples paired off, her nervousness increased.

She wished Jakob hadn't been pressured to accompany her for the snack. What would they talk about? She needed to stop focusing on herself and think about him. How could she ease his heartache?

Soon only a few girls were left; some looked forlorn. Another worry crowded out Sarah's fears about topics of conversation. What if Jakob didn't come for her? Would she have the courage to go down alone?

Then Jakob stood in front of her, even more handsome up close than he had appeared across the room earlier. "Sarah, will you go in to eat the snack with me?"

His question sounded so stiff and formal, her heart sank. But what could she expect? He'd been forced into this out of politeness.

"Thank you." She'd managed to push the words past

the lump in her throat. It wasn't exactly an appropriate answer to his question, but she was so grateful to be rescued from attending as a single, she couldn't put together a coherent thought.

He looked a bit surprised at her answer, but only motioned for her to precede him to the top of the basement steps.

Before they started down the stairs, Sarah tucked her hands behind the folds of her dress, wishing they still followed the old-fashioned custom of holding hands when they went in for the meal.

Beside her, Jakob held out his hand. "Sarah?"

She ducked her head. "You don't have to."

"You'd rather not?"

At his hurt tone, she glanced up. Did he think she was rejecting him? "Oh, Jakob, I'm sorry." She extended her hand.

"Don't feel obligated." He dropped his hand to his side. "I don't want you to feel uncomfortable."

"I'd never feel uncomfortable holding your hand." Heat stung Sarah's cheeks. She sounded so overeager. "I just thought maybe you wouldn't want to hold mine."

Jakob's brow creased. "Why would you think that?"

"Never mind," Sarah mumbled. She lowered her head so Jakob couldn't see the love and joy shining in her eyes when he wrapped his hand around hers. She hoped he couldn't hear her thundering heartbeat or feel the tingling in her palm at his touch.

It had been years since they'd walked hand in hand, but every detail of his fingers, the pressure of his hand, had been imprinted in her memory. The only difference was his hand was larger, stronger, and more calloused from hard work, but as they always had, their hands felt like the perfect fit.

As they descended the steps, Sarah practically floating beside him, the happiest she'd ever been in her life. She struggled to keep her lips from revealing her joy. Then she met Emma's gaze across the room. The anxiety on her sister's face relaxed into a broad smile. Sarah gave Emma only a brief nod, afraid if she smiled back, she wouldn't be able to stop grinning, and everyone would discern her secret.

Jakob let go of her hand to help her into a chair, and Sarah missed the warmth of his hand folded over hers.

They sat in silence for a few minutes, as Sarah had feared they would. Swallowing hard and gathering all her courage, Sarah leaned toward Jakob and whispered, "Thank you for speaking up for me in church this morning."

"*Ach*, it was the least I could do. No Amish would sign a document like that. Certainly not you."

"I appreciated your belief in me. I wish I knew who would have done such a thing."

"It was a cruel trick for sure and certain. Especially when it is done to someone who is always kind to others."

A compliment from Jakob? Sarah wanted to tuck it into her heart and memory to pull it out later, but that would be *hochmut*. She brushed it aside with a wave of her hand. "It was not me I was worried about. Those photographers could have spoiled Emma's entire wedding. I'm so glad she and Sam weren't there to see it, and that you, *Dat*, and *Mammi* were able to convince them to leave."

"You give me too much credit. Your family took care of it."

Jakob had played a big part. He'd been the first to escort the woman out, but Sarah let it drop. He would not want to be praised. That was another thing she admired about him. His dedication to the faith. He always tried to do the right thing, no matter the cost.

Emma, back when she was rebellious, had teased Lydia about Jakob being too stiff and self-righteous. But to Sarah, he had been a wonderful example of someone who lived as God commanded. Sarah had been so busy reminiscing about Jakob's virtues the past few minutes, she'd ignored the actual man sitting beside her. Rebecca's comments from yesterday about Jakob and problems came to mind.

After they had heaped their plates, she leaned closer so nobody could overhear, hoping Jakob couldn't detect the acceleration of her heartbeat. "Is everything all right with you?"

Jakob stared at her, two small lines forming between his brows. Was he angry or puzzled?

Sarah hadn't meant to offend him. Perhaps the problem Rebecca mentioned was a private matter. "I'm sorry. I hope all is well with your health and—and everything else."

"My health is fine as far as I know, and as for everything else, was there something specific you wanted to know?"

"Well, no, it's just that I…" she stumbled over her words. She'd almost said she cared about him. "So everything's all right?"

"It seems to be. The business is going well. It was a

bit rocky after I took over because I didn't have the same skills as my dad, so some people pulled their business."

"But you're a fine woodworker," she burst out.

"*Danke* for saying so, but I'm still learning. It's difficult to pick up techniques when *Dat* struggles to explain in words and can't demonstrate, so I've been apprenticing to two other woodworkers in the evenings when I don't have to care for *Dat*."

"You work so hard. That must be exhausting."

Jakob gave her a grateful glance. "It has been tiring, but I'm learning."

"And caring for your *dat* in addition. That's so *gut* of you."

"No, that's a pleasure." Jakob's face relaxed into a broad smile. "He's always cheerful and wise. Spending time around him helps me grow spiritually."

"How wonderful."

For the first time that afternoon, Jakob gave her a genuine smile. "You would appreciate that. I remember how seriously you took studying for our baptismal classes."

Sarah drew in a sharp breath. She should steer the conversation in another direction before he recalled that he and Lydia were the ones doing the studying. She'd only been listening in.

But Jakob went on. "I could never decide on those nights which I appreciated more—you baking my favorite desserts or watching you, head bent over the *Dordrecht Confession*, a serious expression on your face, as you explained yet another passage that confused Lydia and me."

So he did remember Lydia had been there? But he

also remembered her. And he knew she'd baked those desserts especially for him? How embarrassing!

He said teasingly, "At the time I might have said I preferred the desserts, but now with the passing years, I'm more and more grateful for the spiritual insights you shared. Not everyone studies that hard for their baptism."

Was that admiration in his eyes? Sarah ducked her head. "I can't take credit for that," she protested. "*Mammi* helped me understand the meanings."

"But you took the time to ask her and figure it all out before we met. I never would have learned that much if you hadn't taken the initiative."

"I'm glad I could help at least a little." She was grateful she'd been able to bring something of value to their evening studies when she'd been a third wheel. Lydia and Caleb had been courting, so they should have been spending time alone together. Instead, she sat in on each session—at Lydia's insistence.

A light dawned. Perhaps even then, Lydia had been in love with Caleb and had invited Sarah to study with them to prevent Jakob from getting romantic. Poor Jakob. Had he ever figured out her ruse and been hurt by it?

"Are you all right?" Jakob asked. "You were looking so sad."

"I was just remembering…" She couldn't bring up her questions about Lydia. She needed to deflect the conversation. So many memories crowded in. She grabbed a random one. "Remember the time you offered to teach me how to catch a frog?" She'd been eight, and he'd been twelve.

He laughed. "And you fell headfirst into the creek?"

A sober look crossed his face. "I guess I shouldn't be laughing. You could have drowned with the way you panicked."

"I probably would have if you hadn't saved me." Sarah recalled her relief after his arms closed around her. She'd stopped thrashing and relaxed against him, limp and exhausted.

"You didn't really need to be saved. The water only came up to your waist. You could have stood up and been safe."

"I didn't realize that at the time. I can still remember that horrible fear, the suffocation of my head under water, not being able to breathe."

Jakob had struggled to pull her out; her heavy waterlogged dress had tangled on the rocks. He'd been so patient, talking to her as gently as he had that kitten he'd saved. *Mamm* had been furious about the soaked and torn dress. That was the one and only time she could remember getting into trouble. She tried so hard to be good after that.

"That must have been awful for you. When your dress got snagged, I was afraid I'd never get you out."

"You never showed it. You seemed so brave, and you kept soothing my fears."

"That's what older brothers learn to do—we can't show our own fears. It's not always easy looking after younger siblings."

Younger siblings. That's how he'd always thought of her. She was even younger than his sister Rebecca. Sarah concentrated on swirling a slice of apple into the fruit dip so he couldn't see the distress in her eyes.

Jakob finished everything on his plate and relaxed back in his chair. "We always had fun together, didn't we?"

"Yes, we did," she breathed. Every moment they'd been together had been special. But one memory stood out more than the rest. The incident that had made her fall in love with him. "I don't know if I ever thanked you for helping me save that kitten."

"You still remember that?" Jakob smiled and bit into one of the molasses cookies on his plate.

"Of course, I do." Sarah was too filled with excitement and nervousness to eat, so she only pushed the last piece of fruit around her plate. "You were my hero that day," she said shyly. "I was so scared of blood—and still am—but you knew just what to do."

Jakob's cheeks turned scarlet. "Anyone would have done the same if they'd seen your tears." He gazed off into the distance. "You were always so sweet and tenderhearted when you were little." He turned and studied her.

Sarah lowered her eyes, both out of embarrassment and to prevent him from glimpsing the feelings overflowing in her heart.

"You haven't changed."

A swift, sharp pain shot through Sarah. Yes, he'd complimented her, but it seemed he still saw her as that younger six-year-old sister. She tried to content herself with that. As friends, they could have conversations like this as long as she kept her true feelings hidden. She'd rather have this than the formality and coldness of the past four years.

If only this brief snack with Jakob could last forever.

Chapter Twelve

Sarah was just leaving the *daadi haus* the next morning after dropping off breakfast for *Mammi* and the two men, when Sam and Emma strolled across from the kitchen. Sarah stopped in the doorway to block their entrance. "What are you doing here?" To her dismay, her words came out confrontational.

"Sarah?" Emma stared at her in surprise. "We can't visit *Mammi*? We wanted to thank her for the beautiful quilt. I can't believe she made that with her arthritis so bad most days."

"It is lovely, isn't it?" *Mammi* had made a double wedding ring quilt in shades of peach and turquoise, and only Sarah knew how many painful hours their grandmother had invested in stitching each tiny strip into delicate, interlocking circles.

"So, can we get by?" Emma asked.

"What? Oh, right, you want to see *Mammi*."

"That's what I said." Emma's forehead wrinkled. "Sarah, are you all right?"

"Yes, yes, of course. It's just that *Mammi*, um… She's getting ready to come out."

Now both Sam and Emma were studying her as if she'd gone crazy. And perhaps she had. Keeping secrets from her family was crazy, wasn't it?

Desperate to prevent them from entering, Sarah opened the door and called, "*Mammi*, Sam and Emma are here, but I told them you were coming out."

Emma took the handle of the storm door and started to pull, but Sarah kept her grip on the door. A mini tug-of-war ensued until *Mammi* came shuffling down the hall.

"I'm going over to the kitchen for a cup of coffee," *Mammi* told them. "Would you like to join me?"

"Sure," Emma said, her face still puzzled.

With *Mammi* leading the way and Sarah bringing up the rear, they made their way to the kitchen. After she shut the kitchen door behind her, Sarah leaned back against it with a sigh.

When Emma tilted her head and raised an eyebrow, Sarah said defensively, "It's been tiring." Although that was partially true, her stomach ached from the cover-up.

Her sister's shoulders drooped, and her smile disappeared. "I'm sorry the wedding has been so hard on you."

"Oh, Em, no. It's not that." Not only had she lied, she'd hurt her sister's feelings. "I was happy to help. I still am. In fact, I'll pack up the dishes while you two talk to *Mammi*." The wedding trailer would be returning soon for the supplies so they could be delivered to Sadie Byler's house this afternoon for her Thursday wedding.

"You don't have to, Sarah. Sam and I will take care of things."

"I'm happy to do it." Sarah hurried from the room. The church ladies had stayed last night until the last dish had been washed and dried. All that remained was to pack them into the boxes. Sarah had most of the dish containers ready by the time Emma and Sam reached the basement.

Sam carted benches and chairs upstairs while Emma removed tablecloths and tossed them into the wringer washer. Zeke and Abe clattered downstairs to fold tables and carry them out. When the wedding wagon rattled up the driveway, they all rushed out to help load.

Then Sarah *redded* up the kitchen while Emma mopped the basement floors and *Mamm* cleaned the living room. Sam and the boys helped *Dat* in the barn. By lunchtime, Sarah truly was exhausted. They had plenty of leftover food from the wedding, so she warmed some for lunch and set out pickles, chips, and cake.

She was grateful when *Mammi* loaded a tray to take over to the *daadi haus*. Once *Mammi* was safely out the door, Sarah called the rest of the family to lunch.

Sam's family and relatives had left early that morning so they could get back to work, so Sarah changed all the bedding upstairs and carried the sheets down to wash. Emma had finished the tablecloths and hung them out to dry. Sarah was in the back yard hanging out the last sheet when Rebecca strolled through the fields toward the house.

"I came to see if I could help with the cleaning," she called.

"Perfect timing. The work's all done, and I was about to snack on some of the leftover cake."

Rebecca followed her into the kitchen. "I'm glad you'll be back at school tomorrow. The scholars always behave better when you're around. I wish I had your gift of getting them to cooperate."

"I played with them a lot when they were younger.

Perhaps they think of me more as a playmate than an authority figure." That brought to mind Jakob's comments. She didn't mind if the students classified her as young enough to be one of them, but she'd like to find a way to make Jakob realize she could be more than a little sister.

"Are you all right?" Rebecca asked. "You're looking so wistful."

Sarah forced her mind back to the kitchen. "I'm fine. Would you like some peanut butter delight?"

After they settled at the table with their squares, Rebecca said, "I guess the wedding wore you out?"

"*Jah*, you could say that." Both physically and emotionally. "Weddings are a lot of work."

"But they're fun."

Yes, if you're part of a couple and looking forward to one of your own. For Sarah, they only pointed out her aloneness. Although sitting with Jakob at dinner had been wonderful. Once they'd overcome their stiffness and relaxed, the conversation had flowed. Both of them had ignored their neighbors at the table as they'd told one story after another. It almost seemed they'd gone back to their former friendship. Jakob might not ever love her the way she did him, but she'd be content if they could remain friends.

"Sarah?" Rebecca snapped her fingers in front of Sarah's face. "You looked so dreamy and faraway."

"I'm so sorry. It's just that…"

Rebecca made a face. "I know, I know. You're probably dreaming of your own wedding. So am I."

Her friend had mistaken her preoccupation. Yet Sarah couldn't correct her, or she'd have to explain that she'd been thinking about Jakob. Her heart burdened with untold truths, Sarah turned away to hide her flushed cheeks.

"Sarah, I came here to ask a favor."

"Of course. I'm happy to help."

"Actually, it's about Abner. But first I need to ask you a question about my brother."

Her brother? "What about him?" she asked cautiously.

"You and my brother seemed to be getting along well last night." Rebecca's words were laced with sarcasm. "Did he ask you to be on his side?"

Sarah stared at her. "His side? In what?"

"You didn't discuss me?"

Actually, they hadn't mentioned Rebecca. But she didn't want to hurt her friend's feelings. "We shared old memories, humorous things we did as children."

Rebecca eyed her suspiciously. "When you had your heads together like that, Jakob never mentioned me and what a problem I am?"

"Of course not. Why would he? You're one of the nicest people I know, and I would have told him so if he dared to criticize you."

"Oh, Sarah, you're the sweetest, most loyal friend. I don't deserve a friend as kind as you."

"You most certainly do."

"Perhaps you'd better wait to hear what I have to tell you first."

"Nothing will change my opinion."

Rebecca laid a hand on her arm. "Thank you for that. So back to my brother. I'm sure you know how over-protective Jakob is."

Sarah's heart fluttered at the mention of Jakob's name. "*Jah*, he's a wonderful *gut* brother."

"Sometimes his *caring*—" sarcasm dripped from

the word "—is hard to take. And he's taken a dislike to Abner, so he won't leave us alone together. We can't even have a private conversation without Jakob joining us."

"I'm sure he means well."

"Of course, you'd take his side. But we want to talk about our relationship."

Sarah sucked in her breath. She shared some of Jakob's misgivings about Abner. He belonged to a wilder group of *youngie*, ones who owned cars, computers, and cell phones. "You shouldn't be discussing dating, when he hasn't joined the church yet."

"He'll join this spring." The confidence of Rebecca's tone didn't match the doubtful expression on her face. "It's been hard for him to give up some of his *Englisch* ways."

Would he ever want to? Sarah didn't voice her own concerns. From the lines around Rebecca's eyes, her friend already had plenty of worries. "I'm glad to hear he's planning to join the church."

"He promised me he will, but that isn't what I'm here to talk about. We need some time alone together to talk about that, but with Jakob around…"

"I can see that would be difficult, even though Jakob's well meaning. But perhaps you could take a little time on the way home from a hymn sing."

"That's the problem. He even follows Abner's buggy to and from events. If we pulled over, he would too."

"Oh dear. Have you tried talking to him about it? I'm sure if he understood…"

Rebecca burst out, "He doesn't understand. He hasn't courted anyone since—" She clapped a hand over her mouth. "I'm so sorry."

A knife slashed through Sarah's heart, sharp and

painful, but she struggled to keep a neutral expression. Every time she remembered Jakob courting Lydia, the memories ripped open the old wounds, wounds Rebecca had no idea existed. Her friend knew only that it pained Sarah to remember Lydia's rejection of Jakob. Rebecca often criticized Sarah for being too sensitive to other people's feelings and likely assumed that was why recounting the story upset her.

After a sympathetic glance at Sarah, Rebecca continued, "Anyway, Abner and I would like some time together, so I wondered if we could meet at your house. If we could sit here in the living room, your family will be in and out, so we wouldn't really be alone. But we could talk in private."

Although Sarah couldn't figure out why Rebecca couldn't do the same at home, she didn't want to let her friend down. "I suppose that would be all right."

Rebecca leaned over and gave her a quick hug. "Thank you so much." She jumped up. "I can't wait to tell Abner!" As she left, she said, "Jakob never worries when I'm with you." Then she paused. "Promise me you won't tell him?"

That was an easy promise to make because when would she ever talk to Jakob?

After the door slammed behind Rebecca, Sarah sat at the table for a few minutes, feeling uneasy. Had she just agreed to something that would undermine Jakob? If he followed Abner's courting buggy and wouldn't allow the couple to be alone together, maybe he had good reason. She hoped she wouldn't cause any trouble by helping Rebecca. The last thing she wanted was to hurt or upset Jakob. She vowed to keep a close eye on the couple so Jakob would have no worries.

Chapter Thirteen

The following morning Sarah had to go back to work, so she brought breakfast over for the men before she left. Her grandmother followed her to the door, stepped outside, and pulled it shut behind her.

"Something is going on with those men," she said. "Yesterday when I took dinner over, Herman was badgering Paul to call someone to hook up the electricity."

"Oh, no. *Dat* would be so upset."

Mammi smiled. "Don't worry. I persuaded him not to."

Sarah could only imagine *Mammi*'s persuasion. "That's good."

"Yes, Paul had a battery-operated charger delivered for their phones and computers. Anyway, I got tired yesterday so I went to bed soon after dinner."

"I'm so sorry. I should have checked on you." It had been a long, exhausting day for all of them, especially cleaning up after the wedding the previous day, but all the work and excitement of the past few days would have been especially wearing on *Mammi*.

"I'm not an invalid, Sarah." *Mammi* gave her an exasperated look. "Anyway, those two were on their phones all evening. I couldn't hear what they were saying, but they started whooping and hollering around ten and kept it up until after midnight. I think both of them were dancing around too, judging by the thumping sounds."

"I'm sorry they disturbed you, *Mammi*." If Herman could walk—and dance!—why was he pretending to have a broken leg?

"When I yelled for them to quiet down, they did. I think they'd forgotten I was there. Or else they were too excited to care. This morning when I asked what all the fuss was last night, they both looked at me like I was crazy and only shrugged."

"I need to leave for school," Sarah said, "but we'll have to figure out what's going on." She hurried off so she wouldn't be late, but *Mammi*'s story stayed on her mind all day.

At the end of the school day, Rebecca called to her. "Would it be all right if Abner and I stop by tonight?"

Sarah had been hoping to solve the mystery tonight, but she bit back a sigh and nodded. Rebecca's grateful smile lifted her spirits and made her glad she'd agreed. Her best friend's happiness was more important than trying to get the truth out of Herman.

As soon as Sarah got home, she headed to the *daadi haus*, determined to find out what was going on. Although she felt guilty about sneaking inside, she opened the front door as quietly as she could and tiptoed down the hall.

Herman's voice carried from the living room. "That's right," he said, his voice full of glee, "we got the green light."

Sarah peeked into the living room to see if they had

company, but Herman was talking on his phone. Paul spied her and signaled to Herman.

"Gotta go, but we're ready to get started. Just wanted to give you a heads-up."

After he hung up, Sarah said, "Sounds like you got some good news." She wasn't sure what he meant by green light, when he wasn't out driving, unless he was referring to the car parked beside the house. Paul had pulled it in so it couldn't be seen from the family house, but it would be visible from the road.

"I noticed a car out there." She said it casually, so she wouldn't arouse their suspicions.

"Yeah, Paul rented it today, so he can get around."

"I thought you were in hiding."

"Yep, I am," Herman said, "but he has a lot of work to do on an important project. It's still hush-hush."

Sarah assumed he meant secret. "So I understand you can dance."

Herman looked taken aback for a moment, but then his features settled into an expression of innocence. "Not sure where you got that idea."

A knock sounded on the front door, and they all jumped. Sarah hurried to answer it.

"Rebecca? What are you doing here?" She cringed inside. Her words sounded unwelcoming. "I'm sorry. I'm happy to see you. I only meant…"

"I understand. You can stop apologizing. I know you love me and are delighted to see me."

"*Jah*, I do and I am." Her friend's feelings were more important than the secret she was hiding. Sarah held her arms open in welcome. "Let's start over. I'm happy to see you. Why don't we go over to the house?"

"I don't want to keep you from your company."

"Company?" The sick feeling in her stomach increased. "H-how did you know?"

"I saw a car over there."

"Oh, right. Well, that's, um…" How could she explain Paul's car?

"Look, I only stopped by to see if nine would be too late tonight. Abner has to work until closing."

"I guess that would be all right." Her parents usually went to bed around then. And she'd been planning an early night, but she should help her friend.

"You don't sound too sure."

"No, it's fine. I'm happy to have you."

"Thanks, Sarah." Rebecca's face lit up, then she sobered. "I don't want to keep you from your guests, but I did have something to ask."

Worried Rebecca might hear the men in the living room, Sarah stepped out on the porch and shut the door. "Why don't we go into the kitchen?"

"But you have company."

"It's not important. *Mammi* can take care of them."

Rebecca looked at her oddly and tilted her head as if waiting for an explanation. When none was forthcoming, she sighed.

Knowing Rebecca's weakness for dessert, Sarah distracted her by offering her some. When her friend was settled at the table with a slice of coconut cake, Sarah said, "You needed to ask me something?"

"It's about Jakob. He keeps such a close eye on me, I worry he'll figure out what I'm doing. If he shows up while Abner's here, can you distract him until Abner can slip out the back door?"

Sarah couldn't keep the shock from her face. "Deceive your brother?"

Rebecca sighed. "I knew you wouldn't agree."

Sarah reached for her friend's hand. "I'm worried about you. All this sneaking around, lying to your family—maybe not in words, but in concealing things from them—and…" Sarah stopped speaking as her own words convicted her. Wasn't she doing the exact same thing she was counseling her friend not to do? If she had a clear conscience, Sarah could offer better advice. But how could she ask her friend to do what she herself wasn't doing?

Rebecca hung her head. "I know. But I love Abner, and my family is trying to get me to stop seeing him. I won't give him up."

"Maybe if they got to know him," Sarah suggested, "they'd see he'd make a good boyfriend. Once he joins the church, that is."

Rebecca frowned. "They don't see his potential the way I do; they only see what he's like right now."

"But isn't what he's like right now an indication of what he'll be like in the future?"

"Now you sound like Jakob."

"Your brother used to be good friends with Abner. Perhaps you should heed his counsel."

"It figures you'd side with Jakob. You've always followed him around like a puppy dog and hung on his every word."

Her crush on Jakob was that transparent? Sarah cut another bite of her cake, but the nausea churning in her stomach prevented her from lifting it to her mouth. Had Jakob known it too? His comment at dinner about her baking his favorite desserts showed he'd been aware of her admiration.

Rebecca shoved back her chair. "This was a mistake.

I should have known you'd agree with my family." Her eyes brimming with tears, she rushed toward the door.

Sarah jumped up, almost overturning the bench in her haste. "Wait, Rebecca. Don't leave like this."

But the door slammed behind her friend.

Sarah was still sitting at the table replaying the conversation with Rebecca when *Mamm* entered the kitchen to start dinner. When her mother asked gently what was wrong, Sarah almost burst into tears. If only she could unburden her conscience. But how could she tell *Mamm* she was hiding two men in the *daadi haus*, she'd had a fight with her best friend, her crush on Jakob wasn't a secret, and she'd agreed to help Rebecca disobey her parents?

Rather than answering, Sarah cleared the snack plates from the table and began peeling and chopping potatoes for the stew. She searched for something to say. "It was an adjustment going back to school today after having so much time off for Emma's wedding."

"That would be tiring."

Actually, being at school had been the least stressful time she'd had in the past week. She'd forgotten about everything except math, spelling, and reading. Being in the classroom was a joy. "It was good to be back. I think some of the scholars missed me."

"And I'm sure Rebecca was grateful to have your assistance."

On hearing her friend's name, Sarah choked up. She had to find a way to mend their relationship before tomorrow. With how upset Rebecca had been, Sarah doubted her friend would meet Abner here tonight, so she could clear at least one thing from her conscience.

With so many topics to avoid, Sarah switched the

conversation to Emma's wedding. She and *Mamm* chatted happily until dinnertime. The discussion lasted through the meal, with *Dat* getting teary-eyed whenever they mentioned Emma's name.

"I wish Sam and Emma had been able to stay here for a few months the way most couples do." *Mamm* choked up.

"I do too," Sarah said. But Sam's *onkel* Eli had suffered another heart attack, and until he recovered, Sam needed to care for him and run the farm.

Seeing *Mamm* close to tears, *Dat* changed the subject to an upcoming auction, and the rest of the meal passed in pleasant conversation. After everyone left the kitchen, Sarah prepared plates for the men and slipped out before she did the dishes.

When she entered with their dinner, Herman waved a dismissive hand. "Now that Paul has a car, we won't need that s—"

Paul cut him off. "We appreciate the meals you've fixed us, don't we, Herman?"

He glared until Herman said a grudging, "I guess. But I'd rather have sushi or parathas or, well, anything really. So Paul will make food runs for us."

That would be a relief. So far, *Mamm* hadn't remarked on the amount of food disappearing because they had so many leftovers.

"I couldn't believe no one will deliver this far out," Herman griped. "That's crazy. How do you survive without deliveries?"

Sarah smiled. "We make our meals, so it's never been a problem." Then she took a deep breath. She hated complaining, but she had to deal with the car issue. "Paul, I'm concerned about the car being outside. My friend questioned it, and my family and the neighbors might notice it too. If you're trying to keep your presence secret, it might be better to move it."

"Hmm, I hadn't thought about that."

"Just beyond the two farms up the road, there's a large turnaround." Sarah pointed to the left. "Several commuters park there to catch rides into the city for work, so nobody will mind if you park there."

"I'll do that." Paul got up from his chair. "About how far is it?"

"Maybe a half mile or so."

"What?" Herman exclaimed. "Walk all that way?"

Mammi raised her eyebrows in mock surprise. "Since you can't walk, I don't imagine it'll make a difference to you."

Herman blustered for a few seconds, but then settled down under *Mammi*'s eagle-eyed gaze, and Sarah returned to the kitchen with the full tray.

After she put away the food and washed the dinner dishes, she sat at the kitchen table to work on the next day's lessons for the younger students. Usually she worked at the desk in her bedroom, but tonight the room seemed too empty without Emma. Having her sister sleep there for the week before the wedding made Sarah realize how lonely the room was without her sisters. Even down here, she could barely keep her mind on the work with all the worries whirling in the back of her mind.

A tap at the back door startled her. She turned to see Rebecca peering through the glass. Sarah rushed to the door.

Before Sarah could apologize, Rebecca hugged her. "I'm sorry for what I said earlier. Will you forgive me?"

"Of course. If you'll forgive me for being critical."

"You were trying to be helpful, and I appreciate it, but nobody understands Abner the way I do."

"So he's still coming tonight?" Sarah tried to keep the censure from her words.

Rebecca's starry eyes answered that question. "I'll wait for him on the front porch, so he doesn't knock and disturb your parents."

"But I thought you'd be sitting in the living room."

"I'll bring him right in. Don't fret, Sarah."

Sarah couldn't help worrying. She hadn't asked her parents' permission, she was defying Rebecca's parents and Jakob, and if Abner wasn't as trustworthy as Rebecca supposed… Sarah would share the blame if anything bad happened. Before she could mention her concerns, Rebecca dashed out of the kitchen and slipped out the front door.

A short while later, a loud engine spit and growled up the driveway. Abner's car. Sarah's teeth clenched. Had Abner considered the noisy engine might disturb her parents? If they woke, how would she explain? She hurried into the living room to light the propane lamp. No way would she let the two of them sit in the dark. Then she stood, waiting for them, her anxiety growing as each minute passed. How long did it take for Abner to get out of his car and walk to the porch? Finally, the two of them strolled in the door, holding hands. The dreamy look on Rebecca's face and her *kapp* slightly askew set off alarm bells in Sarah's head. What had she done by agreeing to these meetings?

Following Rebecca's thankful smile and Abner's gruff *danke*, the two of them took separate seats, and Sarah relaxed a little. If they were only going to talk, she could give them some privacy. Although she longed to go to bed, she returned to the kitchen unsure about how much chaperoning to do.

She paced around the kitchen. Should she peek in on them? She didn't want to spy on them, but they needed to realize she took her duties as chaperone seriously. Pulling out a serving platter, Sarah arranged some cake slices on it as an excuse to interrupt them. Before she started down the hall, Abner's engine rumbled out of the driveway, and Sarah sighed in relief.

When Rebecca didn't come out to the kitchen, Sarah hurried down the hall. The living room was empty.

She ran to the front door and pulled it open. Had Rebecca started walking home after Abner left? But why hadn't she said good-bye? Maybe she'd assumed Sarah had gone to bed. Sarah refused to believe the alternative. Rebecca wouldn't have asked to meet here and then sneaked out with Abner.

Sending up a prayer for her friend's safety, Sarah put away the cake slices and finished her lesson plans. As she headed up the stairs to bed, a light tap sounded on the front door. Had Rebecca returned? Sarah rushed to the door and pulled it open, and her heart danced, but then sank.

"Jakob?" Her thoughts raced as she stared at him. What was he doing here so late at night? Had something happened to Rebecca? Sarah's mind flashed back to the night the police came to the door to tell them Emma had been in an accident. *Please help Rebecca to be safe*.

"Sarah, I'm sorry to disturb you so late at night, but I came to pick up Rebecca. I didn't want her walking home alone. Are you both done with your lesson plans?"

"I—I am." Sarah had no idea about Rebecca's. If

Jakob hadn't seen his sister walking home, that meant Rebecca had… Sarah refused to believe her friend could be so dishonest. Though she had no idea what to tell him, she couldn't leave Jakob standing on the doorstep. Pulling the door open wider, she invited him in.

As Jakob stepped into the hall, a flurry of movement behind Sarah startled her. Rebecca breezed down the hall from the kitchen.

"Jakob," she said, "what are you doing here?"

"I came to pick you up."

"Perfect timing. Sarah and I just finished our lesson plans."

Sarah stared at her, mouth open. "But…"

Rebecca flashed her a *don't-you-dare-tell-him* glare, and Sarah stayed silent. She owed her friend a chance to explain before she judged the situation. Perhaps it had all been a misunderstanding.

"I'm glad to hear that." Jakob's words didn't match his grim expression. "Perhaps you could explain why Amos Schrock saw Abner's car here a short while ago."

Rebecca only laughed. "He must have been mistaken. He probably saw that black car parked near the *daadi haus*. It's not easy to tell black cars apart at night."

Sarah bit back a gasp. Since when had Rebecca become such an accomplished liar?

Jakob didn't look convinced and turned toward Sarah, but before he could question her, Rebecca rushed toward her and hugged her.

"Thanks so much for helping me tonight," she said. "I'm sorry I kept you up so late." While Sarah stood there dazed, Rebecca grabbed Jakob's arm. "We should go so Sarah can get some sleep. She's probably still exhausted after Emma's wedding."

With an apologetic glance at Sarah, Jakob let Rebecca drag him to the front door. Sarah trailed behind, still trying to make sense of what had just happened.

"Forgive us both for keeping you up," Jakob said as Rebecca hurried onto the porch. "Sleep well." His friendly smile would have sent her spirits soaring if she hadn't been weighed down with guilt over Rebecca's lies. Sarah had no idea how to tell Jakob the truth without betraying her friend.

Chapter Fourteen

After a restless night, Sarah plodded to the school-house. Rebecca sat at her desk, head bent over her work, scribbling rapidly. She appeared so engrossed in her work, Sarah was reluctant to interrupt her.

A short while later, after their usual greetings, the scholars tumbled into the schoolhouse, and lessons began. Throughout the day, Rebecca avoided Sarah's eyes. Rather than staying inside to talk at lunchtime or recess, Rebecca hurried outside. She made a show of keeping a careful watch on the children, but Sarah could tell she was deliberately evading her. When the last scholar left at the end of the day, Rebecca grabbed her satchel.

"Rebecca," Sarah began hesitantly, but either her friend didn't hear or was ignoring her, because Rebecca hustled out the door, letting it bang shut behind her. The tears that had threatened all day pooled in Sarah's eyes. How could she make things right between them if Rebecca refused to acknowledge her? Was it a guilty conscience that made her friend so reluctant to speak to her? Or maybe Rebecca was afraid Sarah would condemn her. Although Sarah had been shocked and hurt by her friend's behavior last night, she wouldn't judge her, but she did want to hear Rebecca's reasons for lying. Perhaps with church being at the Zooks' house, she could find a few minutes alone with her friend. She prayed God would give her an opportunity to discuss things with Rebecca.

On Sunday morning Sarah dressed hastily and hurried down to start breakfast. *Mamm* joined her, and after drinking a few sips of coffee, she slogged to the cupboard and took out the dishes, her face was downcast.

"What's the matter, *Mamm*?" Sarah asked as she carried the sticky buns to the table.

Mamm cradled her arms as if holding a baby. "Last Sunday during church, I held Elizabeth while she slept. This Sunday my arms will feel so empty."

Sarah wanted to hug her mother, but neither of her parents believed in expressing physical affection in public, so she contented herself with patting *Mamm*'s shoulder.

Dat also seemed moody. Perhaps he missed the twins too. After a rocky start when they were born, he'd taken to grandfathering and loved spending time with the babies.

Mammi bustled into the kitchen. "What's with all the glum faces this morning? It's a church Sunday; you should be rejoicing."

"Last church Sunday we were all together." *Mamm*'s chin wobbled.

Easing herself into her chair, *Mammi* said, "We're all together this Sunday too."

"I think *Mamm*'s missing Emma, Lydia, and the twins."

"The point of raising children is to teach them to

live on their own," *Mammi* said. "So you did your job, ain't so?"

Mamm nodded.

"And you still have three children sitting at this table." *Mammi* looked at each person in turn. "Be grateful for the ones you have, rather than pining for the ones who aren't around."

Following that pronouncement, every head bowed. When they finished praying, *Dat* said, "I'm very grateful for my family seated at the table here." He glanced at *Mammi*. "But I would enjoy seeing my other *dochters* and the *bopplis* again. Perhaps we could visit Emma and Lydia?"

Mamm's eyes shone. "What a wonderful *gut* idea. Maybe next Saturday?"

Dat shook his head. "Next weekend we need to visit my *Aenti* Ruth. She's been doing poorly, but why don't we hire a van for the following Saturday?"

Faces around the table brightened, and Sarah smiled at *Mamm*'s giddiness. Seeing Emma and Lydia meant so much to her. *Would she miss me that much if I were gone?* When they were growing up, the family revolved around the two older girls, and Sarah had faded into the background. Even with her sisters gone, she still often felt overlooked, as if she were a cooking pot or milk pail—essential to the daily functioning of the family, but often discounted and unnoticed. No one would pay attention unless those items went missing, and even then, they were easily replaced.

Mamm's smile stretched across her face as they washed the dishes, and *Dat* had a cheerful grin when he went outside to hitch up the team. Sarah turned her discouragement about Rebecca over to God and thanked

Him for His blessings. She would enjoy visiting her sisters. She missed them too, and she needed to get over comparing herself with them.

Because the Zooks' house was less than a mile away, Sarah walked rather than rode with her parents. Zeke and Abe went with her, but they sprinted ahead, ran in circles around her, and urged her to walk faster. They kept her so busy, she barely had time to think about the upcoming talk with Rebecca.

After they arrived, Rebecca greeted her, as did Mary Zook and the other church ladies, but her friend once again refused to meet her eyes. Rebecca slipped away before Sarah could ask about talking in private later. With so many women bustling around the kitchen, they'd never be able to have a private conversation.

All through the sermons, Sarah concentrated on the ministers' words, but that didn't stop her from sneaking glances at Jakob or worrying about Rebecca. After the service ended, her friend avoided her. Whenever Sarah entered in the kitchen, Rebecca slipped out to put food on the tables. If Sarah carried out a platter, Rebecca rushed into the kitchen.

Sarah left the church meal with a heavy heart, determined to talk to Rebecca at the hymn sing that night. She spent the afternoon rehearsing what she'd say and walked to the hymn sing a half hour before it began, hoping to catch Rebecca alone before anyone arrived.

Mary Zook answered the door. "Sarah, you're here early. I expect you were hoping to spend time with Rebecca, but she's been in her room, suffering from a headache."

"*Ach*, I'm sorry to hear that."

"I'd say go up to visit with her, but she's sound

asleep. I figured it's best to let her sleep. Perhaps she'll feel better before everyone arrives tonight. And Jakob is helping his *dat* get ready for bed, so he'll be a while."

Sarah regretted her impulsiveness in coming over so early. "I'm happy to help you set up for the hymn sing."

"That's kind of you." Mary strode to the kitchen, Sarah in her wake. "Perhaps you could arrange slices of pie on these platters."

Sarah cut pie while Mary squeezed lemons. Jakob's mother spoke little as she prepared the lemonade, but as they filled plates with cookies, she studied Sarah.

"Is everything all right?" she asked.

Her kind and gentle manner invited confidences, but two of Sarah's concerns were about Rebecca, one was about Jakob, and for the last she'd been bound to secrecy. All of these burdens were getting too heavy to bear, but she could share them with no one.

When she didn't answer, Mary said, "I expect you're all tired after the wedding. Those are always a lot of work."

"That's so," Sarah agreed, then seized on that as a topic of conversation. "It was lovely having Emma and Lydia at home. I hadn't realized how much I missed them until they arrived, but now…"

"It does get lonely. I remember when my sisters got married. I was the youngest girl of five. I missed my brothers too, but the bedroom seemed so empty after my last sister's wedding."

"That's exactly how I feel." Sarah had always loved Jakob's mother, but now she felt an even closer bond. "And *Mamm* really misses the babies."

"*Ach*, that must be so hard having those darling twins living so far away. I'm looking forward to grandchildren. They are the joy of life. Your *mamm* is blessed."

She stopped working and stared off into the distance. "That joy may be a long way off for me. I wonder if my Jakob will ever marry."

Sarah ducked her head and busied herself with setting out more cookies so her eyes wouldn't betray her sorrow that Lydia was the cause for his singleness or reveal her own longing to be Jakob's wife. An impossible dream.

By the time they'd set out the desserts, buggies were pulling into the driveway, and *youngie* streamed into the house. The boys took their places on one side of the tables, and the girls filled in the other side. Sarah tried to save a space for Rebecca, who hadn't come down yet, but someone else squeezed into it. When Rebecca shuffled downstairs, looking pale and drawn, she sat at the opposite end of the table.

Sarah was relieved when the singing began. Lifting her head as well as her voice, she joined in, focusing on each word and the message behind the songs.

They were starting on the third hymn when Jakob arrived, tired lines chiseled around his eyes and mouth. Sarah wished she could ease his exhaustion. His presence across the table encouraged her to sing louder. She loved watching him; he sang with such enthusiasm, his chest rising and falling, his deep bass voice resounding through the room.

Sarah forced herself to look at each of the boys across from her, but her gaze kept returning to Jakob. She hoped the others wouldn't notice.

When they took a break, Jakob came up behind her. "I'm glad you're here tonight, Sarah."

"Thank you. I always enjoy hymn sings at your house." Mainly because she had an uninterrupted view of Jakob. Because he was older than the rest of the *youngie*, he came to hymn sings irregularly, although with him supervising Rebecca's courting, he seemed to be attending more often.

Sarah picked up two cookies and moved down for some lemonade, but Jakob remained beside her. Her hand shook as she picked up the pitcher, and he reached out and took it from her.

"That's heavy. Let me pour it for you."

Was he being solicitous or treating her like a little sister who couldn't pour her own drink? Sarah decided she didn't care; she was just happy to have him close.

As she moved aside so others could get food, Jakob followed her. "*Mamm* said you walked over here. We don't like to think of you alone in the dark, so I can take you home afterwards."

Sarah's pulse skittered at the thought of a buggy ride with Jakob. She'd always dreamed of him asking to drive her home. Now he had, but he was only doing it to be nice, the way he'd come after Rebecca the other night. And because his mother had asked him to. Not the romantic request she'd longed for. Still, she was grateful to have this chance to ride with him.

Jakob glanced over her head, and his lips tightened. Sarah followed his gaze to where Rebecca stood close to Abner. His hand tensed on the cup he was holding, and his sigh conveyed exasperation and disappointment. "I wish I knew what to do about those two," he murmured.

Sarah's feelings mirrored his. She had no idea what to do about them either, although with Rebecca avoiding her, she might not have to deal with the couple meeting at her house.

The break ended too soon for Sarah. She would have

been content to stand near Jakob the rest of the evening. After everyone returned to their places, the hymns began again, Sarah's heart sang along with her lips. She enjoyed each tune and paid attention to the words, but for the first time ever, she was eager for the evening to end so she could spend time alone with Jakob in his courting buggy.

As people said their good-byes and couples paired up for the ride home, Sarah stood to one side, waiting for Jakob to finish his duties as host. Rebecca remained glued to Abner's side, disappointing Sarah. She'd have no chance to talk to her friend.

Jakob made his way over to the couple. "Good to see you tonight, Abner," he said, putting a friendly arm around Abner's shoulders and steering him toward the front door. "Let me see you out. Rebecca's had a bad headache all day, so *Mamm* wants her to go straight to bed."

Fists clenched, Rebecca stood near the foot of the stairs, glaring, as Jakob escorted Abner out the door. Then she whirled around and pounded up the stairs. Sarah longed to go after her, but after what had happened between them, Rebecca wouldn't want her company.

"Why so glum, Sarah?" Jakob said as he walked past to say his good-byes to other guests. "I hope Rebecca didn't allow her annoyance with me to affect your friendship."

Sarah was relieved he kept moving rather than waiting for an answer. She had no desire to tell him what had caused the rift between her and Rebecca.

After the last guest left, Jakob approached her. "Thanks for waiting. Are you ready to go?"

The lines on his face had deepened, and Sarah hated to see him go to the trouble of hitching up the horse. "You look tired. You don't have to do this."

"I'm happy to."

While Jakob went outside for the buggy, Sarah went into the kitchen to help his mother clean up.

"Rebecca should be doing this rather than you," Mary Zook said.

"But she has a headache," Sarah reminded her.

Mary sighed. "It's not only a headache that's bothering her. She's been in a bad mood for the past few days. I wish I knew what was ailing her."

Sarah had a good idea, but she kept her knowledge to herself. That was Rebecca's responsibility to confess to her parents.

They'd finished drying the last of the dishes by the time Jakob returned. "Are you ready to go, Sarah?"

She nodded and turned to Mary Zook. "Thank you so much for having me."

"It was a pleasure as always, dear."

Her genuine smile warmed Sarah's heart. Mary had become almost like a second mother to her, and Sarah hoped the breach with Rebecca wouldn't distance her from Rebecca's mother or her brother.

Chapter Fifteen

Sarah walked beside Jakob to the buggy, every nerve in her body zinging. Twice his sleeve brushed hers, sending her pulse soaring. Being so aware of his every move took up so much of her energy, she had none left to speak. Once he'd helped her into the buggy and the tingling from the touch subsided, Sarah started to worry they'd sit in awkward silence the whole way home. She'd been nervous at the wedding dinner, but they'd ended up chattering nonstop about childhood memories. They'd shared so many happy times. Surely she could find a few to keep the conversation going until they reached home.

Rather than clicking to the horse, Jakob stared up at the night sky. "Isn't it beautiful tonight?"

Overhead stars spangled the blackness of the night sky. Taking a deep breath of crisp fall air, Sarah released the tension constricting her lungs and throat. She'd been so busy thinking of herself and her own fears, she'd forgotten to appreciate the beauty of God's creation or to consider Jakob's feelings. *Lord, please help me to be grateful for Your blessings and to think more of others than my own concerns.*

"It's gorgeous," she said. "Seeing the stars always reminds me of God's greatness."

Jakob smiled at her. "That was my first thought too. He has given us so much to be thankful for."

Their hearts in unison, they were silent as Jakob started the horse down the driveway. Sarah savored the shared moment and stopped worrying about conversation. They rode in silence, drinking in the cool night air and enjoying the stars.

Sarah regretted the briefness of the ride. If she and Jakob had been courting, he might have traveled down some side roads to lengthen their trip, but he had taken her straight home. When he pulled into her driveway, though, he leaned a little closer, a serious expression on his face.

"Sarah, I have a question for you."

The pitter-pattering of her heart increased to thumping drumbeats. Could it be? Would he ask if he could court her? She struggled not to look too eager.

Jakob pinched his lips together a few times and seemed to be struggling for words. Sarah silently urged him to speak.

Finally, he took a deep breath and said, "I'm concerned about Rebecca."

Sarah's hopes smashed into tiny pieces. She struggled to concentrate on what he was saying, to turn her attention from courting to Rebecca.

"I'm glad the hymn sing was at our house because it kept Rebecca home tonight. I know she wanted Abner to stay after the hymn sing, so she's probably furious with me."

Yes, her friend had made that quite obvious.

Jakob continued, "I thought with you two being best friends, you might have some insights into the situation and some influence on her behavior."

Sarah almost blurted out that they were no longer friends, but then she would need to explain why. Something she couldn't do. Instead she opted to tell him a different truth, although she might be risking their tentative friendship. "I know you want to keep her safe, but I think Rebecca resents being watched and followed."

"If you knew what I know about Abner, you'd keep a close eye on your sister."

"I understand. It must be hard seeing them spend time together if you don't trust him."

"Exactly. You do understand." His smile wrapped her in the warmth of acceptance and companionship.

"Of course, I do. I worry about her too." Sarah disliked disturbing the closeness she'd established with Jakob, but she needed to make a point, so he could see his sister's side. "I've found in teaching school, sometimes if you monitor children's behavior too closely, they act out even more. Rebecca isn't a child, but—"

"You think that's what she's doing?"

"I'm not positive, but I suspect she's trying to assert herself and prove her independence."

Jakob nodded. "She's definitely doing that."

"I know." Jakob would be shocked to know how far his sister had gone to gain her freedom. "It's not easy, but maybe if you backed off a bit, Rebecca would realize the truth. Right now, she's so busy championing Abner against others' criticisms, she hasn't taken time to evaluate his character for herself."

"That's true," he agreed, "but I'm worried if I leave them alone, Rebecca will find out about Abner's true nature in an awful and irrevocable way."

"Maybe we need to trust God to protect her and open her eyes." Sarah hoped she wasn't setting her friend up for a terrible heartache. "Perhaps by following her around, you're preventing her from discovering the truth."

Jakob groaned. "I can't believe this. I said almost those exact same words to Lydia when she was chasing after Emma."

Sarah squeezed her eyes shut at the reminder of Jakob's relationship with her older sister. She and Jakob had been getting closer. Yet with one sentence, he'd sent her hopes plunging.

"Sarah? Are you all right?"

How could she answer that truthfully?

"I'm sorry," Jakob said. "I didn't mean to remind you of that sad time."

It had been painful for him too. "Yes, it was a dark time." Emma's rebellion and then her accident had been devastating. "But God brought us through." Sarah pushed aside the other memories that had caused her pain—seeing Lydia and Jakob together—a pain that remained unresolved.

Jakob turned toward her, a question burning in his eyes. "Do you think that's what I'm doing? Causing Rebecca to rebel more?"

Sarah tried to be gentle in her response. "I know you mean well, but you may be."

"I was afraid of that." Jakob rubbed his forehead. "Thank you for your honesty. I've always admired you for that. You always tell the truth, but you do it in a gentle and caring way."

If he knew how many secrets she was hiding, he never would have said that.

"Would you do me a favor?"

Anything, anything at all, she longed to answer. She

hoped her "I'd be happy to" sounded kind rather than overeager or desperate.

"Rebecca trusts your judgment. Could you do your best to steer her away from Abner?"

She had little influence over Rebecca at the moment, and if she and her friend reconciled, Sarah would need to tread carefully in giving advice or criticizing Abner. But how could she resist the pleading look in Jakob's eyes? "I'll try."

Much of the tension melted from Jakob's face. "I knew I could count on you."

Sarah was glad she could ease some of his distress, but she longed to be more than a dependable friend.

The smile that always tripped Sarah's pulse spread across his face, the joyful one that crinkled the laugh lines around his eyes. "It's been so helpful to talk to you."

"I always enjoy spending time with you." As soon as the words were out, Sarah regretted saying them.

But Jakob surprised her. "Really? I figured you wouldn't be interested in spending time with an old man like me."

"You're not old," Sarah protested.

Jakob laughed. "Well, in that case," he said, "since neither of us is dating anyone and we have a good time when we're together, would you want to go to some of the group activities as friends?"

She'd love to be more than friends, but spending any time at all with Jakob would be wonderful. She choked back her eager *yes* and replaced it with a demure, "That would be nice. It's lonely going on my own."

Jakob's face relaxed into a smile. "I wasn't sure you'd agree, but I'm so glad you did. I've been lonely too. I'm older than most of the *youngie* and often feel out of place, but you're younger, so you belong."

Once again, he'd reminded her of her youthfulness, her little sister status. Four years was not a large difference at all, but how could she convince him of that?

"So, would you like to go to the mystery supper together next Saturday? I could pick you up around five."

"That sounds like fun." Sarah thanked him for the ride, then had to restrain herself from skipping across the lawn. She didn't want to let him know how happy his invitation had made her, and she wanted him to forget how young she was.

Jakob waited in the driveway until she opened the front door. She turned and waved before she shut the door. She could hardly believe they'd be going out next weekend. He'd made it clear it wasn't a date, but that didn't dim Sarah's happiness. For now, she'd be content to be friends, and maybe in time...

The next week passed in a blur marked by a flurry of anticipation over her upcoming date with Jakob, working with *Mammi* to figure out what the men were up to, and dealing with Rebecca's ongoing hostility. The friction between the two friends increased each day until Rebecca was barely civil even when they needed to discuss lesson plans or discipline problems.

Sarah tried to smooth things over, but the tension only increased. Perhaps God had sent this as a lesson to show her that hiding secrets hurt those around you. How could she expect Rebecca's honesty when she was harboring secrets of her own? As the Scripture verse admonished, she needed to take the log from her own eye before trying to take a speck out of her friend's.

Sometimes people kept secrets when they'd rather tell the truth—maybe out of shame, or to avoid hurting someone else, or to protect others. Sarah, who had always prided herself on being honest, had used all three as excuses in the past few weeks.

Lord, please give me the wisdom to deal with these secrets I'm harboring. Show me the way to be open and transparent about everything without hurting anyone. And please, please help me find a way to regain my friendship with Rebecca. If there's anything I can do to mend the relationship, make it clear.

On Friday afternoon as they were leaving the schoolhouse, Rebecca asked in a small, hesitant voice, "Would it be all right if I walk home with you?"

Too surprised to answer, Sarah only stared at her. Then she nodded. "Of course."

They were silent on the walk as Sarah waited for Rebecca to speak. Her friend cleared her throat several times and appeared about to say something, but never did. Once they were settled at the kitchen table with bowls of cracker pudding, Sarah broke the silence.

"Rebecca? I'm sorry I was critical of you."

Her friend held up her hand. "No, I'm the one who needs to apologize." Her face crumpled, and she buried her head in her hands. "I'm so sorry I lied." Her voice came out muffled. "Will you forgive me?"

"Of course."

"And for being so cruel this past week?" Rebecca sounded on the verge of tears.

Sarah reached out and set a hand on her shoulder. "For everything, Rebecca. You don't need to list your faults. I have my own I need to ask forgiveness for as well."

Rebecca lifted her head, her eyes wet with tears. "No,

you don't. You've been loving and kind while I've been fighting my conscience and acting nasty."

"But I had a critical attitude," Sarah admitted. "Will you forgive me?"

"Always, dear friend. Although I've never known you to do anything to cause hurt."

Sarah swallowed hard. She wished that were so, but her conscience told her otherwise. Right now, she needed to reassure Rebecca that their friendship remained undamaged. "I'm so glad we can put all this behind us. I've missed talking with you all week."

Rebecca's eyes shone with tears. "Me too. You don't know how hard it was ignoring you all week when all I wanted to do was pour out my heart."

"I'm listening," Sarah said with a smile.

"And I'm grateful." Rebeca gazed up at the ceiling as if the answers to her problems could be found there. "I don't know what to do. Jakob and my parents are against me dating Abner."

"Do you know why?"

Rebecca shook her head. "I've never asked, and to be honest, I don't really want to know. They don't understand Abner the way I do. Nobody does."

"But maybe as outsiders they've seen things that make them worried."

Her friend heaved a sigh. "Look, Sarah, I don't need you to take their side. I need someone on my side. Can you let me talk without interrupting?"

Sarah nodded, scooped up a spoonful of cracker pudding, and slid it into her mouth. The creaminess melted on her tongue. Keeping her mouth full would prevent her from asking questions or offering advice.

"I overheard *Mamm* and Jakob talking. They're

counting on you to convince me to stop dating Abner, but I'm not giving him up. I want to make that perfectly clear. Do you understand?"

Sarah used her fingers to pinch her lips together before she nodded, making Rebecca giggle.

"I didn't mean you couldn't say anything," her friend said.

"I don't want to make any mistakes." Sarah clapped a hand over her mouth. "Oops." She was rewarded by Rebecca's usual wide smile. A smile that cemented over the cracks in their friendship and signaled they were best friends again.

"Abner has been dealing with some tough situations at home and work." Rebecca's mouth tightened. "He's a private person, so I don't feel right sharing them with anyone else, because he says I'm the only one he trusts enough to tell. I'm also the one who's helping him stay on the right path."

Sarah might have her lips sealed, but she couldn't prevent a skeptical look from crossing her face. Rebecca spotted it and stopped talking.

"I'm sorry," Sarah said. "I didn't mean to doubt you. I just remember my *dat* telling us, 'If anyone tells you you're the only one who can save him, point him to God.' It's—" At Rebecca's frown Sarah shut her mouth. Not commenting was harder than she'd expected.

Rebecca took several bites of her dessert, and Sarah wondered if she'd ever finish her story. She mimed locking her mouth and throwing away the key, and it was Rebecca's turn to look skeptical, but after a minute she began again.

"Your *dat* may be right, but I've been a good influence on Abner. No one can save him but God, of course, but I convinced him to join the church. I know we shouldn't be courting until he joins, but he has reasons for waiting. I'm so glad we'll be starting baptismal classes next May. Then my family can't oppose our relationship."

Sarah scraped the last dabs of pudding from her bowl to hide her dismay. How genuine was Abner's faith if he had to be talked into joining?

"Anyway, if you've promised my brother to keep Abner and me apart, I want you to know you can't do it."

Sarah might not have any influence, but God could do anything. *Please, dear Lord, keep Rebecca safe and work in Abner's heart.* She stood and carried her bowl to the sink. "Would you like more pudding?"

"Let me finish this bowl first, and then I'll see. I've been so busy talking I've only eaten a few bites."

A strange buzzing came from Rebecca's satchel. She opened it and pulled out a cell phone. "It's Abner. I won't talk long." Getting up from the bench, she walked down the hall, leaving Sarah staring after her.

A cell phone? Rebecca had a cell phone? Her friend hadn't joined the church yet, the way Sarah had, but Rebecca's father was even stricter than her own *dat*. She couldn't imagine how Rebecca's parents would feel if they found out.

The murmur of her friend's voice came from the living room, but Sarah couldn't make out any words. So she wouldn't be tempted to eavesdrop, Sarah washed her bowl and started dinner. She was peeling potatoes when Rebecca returned to the kitchen.

"Sarah, I know you probably don't trust me after what happened last time, but Abner wants to tell me about a man who's offered him a job. He's so excited. Could he come here for a little while this evening? He can't stay long because he has to meet his new employer tonight."

Rebecca's tearful plea touched Sarah's heart, and against her better judgment, she agreed.

"Thank you, Sarah. I'll text him now." Her thumbs bounced up and down on the screen. "I can't tell you how much this means to me. To us. This could be a whole new start for Abner."

When Abner arrived after dinner, Sarah invited him into the living room where Rebecca was waiting. Then she hesitated in the doorway. Should she go or stay? Maybe she should get to know him better. Perhaps Jakob and his parents had misjudged Abner.

"Sarah, Abner doesn't have much time. He has an interview tonight," Rebecca reminded her.

Taking that as a cue she should leave, Sarah retreated to the kitchen to wash the dishes. As she had the last time Abner was here, Sarah vacillated between chaperoning and giving the couple their privacy. After ten minutes she padded down the hall to ask if they'd like a snack.

She stopped before reaching the doorway. Although their words were unclear, there was no mistaking the fact they were arguing. She wouldn't interrupt them now. Less than five minutes later, Abner's car roared down the driveway. Sarah breathed a sigh of relief that her chaperoning duties were over. She headed down the hall to talk to Rebecca. Her friend might need some comforting after her argument with Abner.

Once again, the living room was empty.

Her heart plummeting, Sarah sank onto the couch. She'd trusted Rebecca. Had the whole apology been a ruse? No, it couldn't have been. She'd seemed genuinely repentant. But Rebecca had tricked her. Twice.

Chapter Sixteen

Sarah sat in the living room for a long while, trying to decide what to do. Should she go to the Zooks and tell them about Rebecca, or should she mind her business and follow the advice she'd given Jakob to allow Rebecca her freedom. Sarah prayed for her friend, asking God to keep her safe from harm and bring her back into harmony with her family.

When Sarah rose early the next morning to do her chores, Rebecca was still on her mind, so she prayed as she worked. While she was washing the breakfast dishes, a light rapping on the window startled her. Rebecca stood at the back door, and Sarah motioned for her to come in.

"I can't stay long," Rebecca said, "but I wanted to apologize for last night."

Remembering how her friend had apologized yesterday and then betrayed her trust, Sarah was wary about being taken advantage of again. "Before you ask, I need to tell you that I can't agree to let you meet Abner here again."

"I didn't intend to ask. I wanted to tell you why I left last night. Abner had that job interview and needed to leave, but he said he wouldn't go unless I went with him. I didn't want him to miss such an important opportunity."

"I wish you'd told me. I worried about you."

Rebecca hung her head. "Abner was so nervous, he was clinging to my hand. I feared if I let go, he'd change his mind about the interview. I wish he had."

When Sarah stared at her in surprise, Rebecca burst out, "Everything's such a mess, but I can't talk now because *Mamm* wants to leave for quilting circle. I only wanted to let you know I was all right. I was going to tell you last night, but…" Tears filled Rebecca's eyes. "I'll explain later. But will you forgive me for last night?"

Sarah wanted to mouth an automatic *yes*, but she had such a jumbled mass of feelings inside to sort out. Yet it was not her place to judge her friend's actions; only God could do that. And she needed to forgive Rebecca the way she wanted God to forgive her. *Lord, help me to think first of Rebecca rather than my own hurt and give me a forgiving heart.* Peace flowed over her. "I forgive you," she said, taking her friend's hands.

"Thank you, Sarah. I need to talk to you about Abner and—" her voice broke "—something else." She glanced up at the clock. "I have to run." She rushed out the door and tore across the lawn.

Knowing Rebecca had arrived home safely last night eased some of Sarah's worries, and she tried not to fret over the mess Rebecca had mentioned. Evidently something had gone wrong last night. Sarah turned it all over to God as she did her chores and allowed the anticipation of seeing Jakob fill her mind and heart.

The day dragged as Sarah glanced at the clock every few minutes, willing the hands to inch along faster.

Finally, at four o'clock she went upstairs to get ready. Then she helped *Mamm* fix dinner for the family, but her thoughts kept straying to Jakob.

"Sarah!" *Mamm*'s sharp tone alerted her to the pot boiling over on the stove.

Sarah snatched a potholder and removed the bubbling pot.

"I'll clean this up," *Mamm* said. "I'm not sure you can handle paying attention that long." She softened her stern words with a smile. "Why don't you go sit in the living room to wait?"

Because I need to keep busy so the time passes more quickly. "I'll do that if you're sure you don't need my help."

Mamm took the pot from her and set it on to simmer. "With the kind of help you've been so far, I think I'll be better off on my own."

Sarah bit her lip. "I'm sorry."

With a laugh, *Mamm* shooed her from the kitchen. "Your mind's on other things tonight. Go and enjoy yourself at the Mystery Supper."

Sarah could hardly wait. Mystery Suppers were always fun, and spending a whole evening with Jakob would be a dream come true. She paced back and forth in front of the living room window so she'd spot Jakob arriving. Finally, he pulled into the driveway. Although he was five minutes early, it felt as if he were an hour late.

Before he could get out of the buggy, she opened the front door and started to race across the lawn. Then remembering her resolve to appear more mature, she slowed down and walked with dignity and grace. But Jakob's welcoming smile lit a fuse inside, and she returned it with a smile so broad her cheeks ached.

"This will be so much fun," Sarah said as she settled

onto the seat beside him. "I hope I can figure out what some of the mystery food is."

Jakob laughed. "My guesses are usually wrong, so I'm expecting to eat my dessert first and main dish last. I only hope I end up with some silverware at the beginning of the meal."

"It's funny to watch other people eat without silverware, but not so humorous when it happens to you."

"I probably shouldn't have asked you to this…" Jakob said.

All the joy and excitement drained from Sarah. He regretted coming with her tonight.

"…that is, if I hope to make a good impression on you."

He cared about what she thought about him? Her spirits soared.

"I'm glad we're old friends and can be comfortable with each other."

Sarah's emotions had gone down, then up, and then down again in a few seconds. Would it always be such a roller coaster ride each time she was with Jakob? She had to stop tying her mood to his every word. She'd always found peace by thinking of the other person rather than herself and her feelings. Why was that so hard when she was with Jakob? It shouldn't be if she cared about him. His needs should come first. *Dear Lord, please help me to put this relationship in proper perspective, to be grateful for the friendship Jakob offers, to let go of my preoccupation with my own feelings, and instead concentrate on being a blessing to others.*

"Why so quiet?" Jakob asked.

"I was thinking." She couldn't share those thoughts with him. To change the subject, she seized on the first topic that came to mind. "Is Rebecca coming tonight?"

A cloud of sadness descended over Jakob's face, making Sarah sorry she'd asked. "I suggested the four of us could ride to this Mystery Supper together, but I'm sure you can imagine her reaction."

Yes, Sarah could picture Rebecca's face when Jakob made that suggestion.

He continued, "I guess it wasn't a wise idea to invite her, but she seemed even more unhappy to find out I was taking you."

Of course, she'd be upset. She'd assume the two of them were plotting against her. "I'm sure she thinks you and I will work together to break up her and Abner."

"Oh, Sarah, I'm sorry. I didn't mean to damage your friendship with Rebecca. You're probably right about her interpretation."

"So she'll be coming with Abner?"

"I don't think so. I believe the two of them had a falling out. I expected to be happy if they broke up, but I hadn't considered how it would affect Rebecca. I've never seen her so depressed."

"Oh, I'm so sorry. But if Abner isn't a suitable person for her to date, perhaps it's for the best."

"I suppose so, but it's hard to watch her hurting and not to be able to do anything to help."

Sarah's heart went out to Rebecca. From the little her friend said this morning, it seemed her eyes had been opened to many things about Abner that didn't make him an ideal husband. To have her hopes and dreams dashed like that would be devastating. "It can be hard to accept that the person you're dating isn't the right person for you."

"That's for sure and certain," Jakob agreed.

Sarah wished she hadn't brought up this topic. He'd

discovered the truth about her sister Lydia the hard way—when she'd turned down his marriage proposal. That's an agony he'd never forget. At least Rebecca and Abner's relationship hadn't progressed that far, although Rebecca acted as if she expected to marry him in the future.

"Speaking of Rebecca," Jakob said, "I have a favor to ask."

"Of course." She'd do anything. Anything at all.

"I know the two of you have a lot of work, but could you send her home earlier? These late nights are hard on her. She was dragging around this morning, exhausted, barely able to do her chores. Some of that may be because of her fight with Abner, but she struggled with a headache last weekend."

How could she tell him Rebecca's tiredness had no connection to the schoolwork? She'd promised Rebecca she wouldn't tell Jakob, but now she regretted making that promise.

"Maybe you could encourage her to stay after school for an hour or so each day to get the work done."

"That would make sense." *If Rebecca truly needed to plan lessons.* But other than tailoring her lessons to fit different students' needs and learning styles, Rebecca had been teaching the same lessons for the past few years. She would only need a short time to go over the plans and put her supplies in order, unless she came up with a new activity or idea, the way Sarah had with the flash cards she'd made last week. And Sarah liked to come up with new lesson plans to reach the reluctant learners.

"I'm so glad I can talk to you about my sister's problems and know you care about her too."

Yes, they had a shared interest in his sister and a

string of childhood memories tying them together, but Sarah yearned for a deeper connection. One that went well beyond friendship.

"We're here," Jakob announced as they pulled into the Fishers' driveway. "Are you ready for a crazy meal?"

Sarah smiled as he helped her down from the buggy, wishing he wouldn't let go of her hand—the warmth and strength and peace it brought, along with a rush of other emotions that made her giddy.

They reached the front door and so did several other couples who were giggling about their mistakes at the last Mystery Supper. They all headed to the Fishers' basement, where tables had been set up around the room. The married couples who were acting as servers handed each of them a menu as they arrived.

Sarah glanced over the list:

Squishy Mortar
Soapy Suds
Jam's Helper
Puddle Muddle
Crazy Mix-up
Annoying Dripper
Decision Points
High Rise
Dieter's Delight
Single Dipper
Whipper Snappers
Scaredy Cat
Root Canal
Arctic Chill
Fire Starter

"We have to pick five items for the appetizer," Sarah said. "I'm going to guess Annoying Dripper is a spoon, Dieter's Delight is water, High Rise might be a fork or knife. I'm not sure what any of the others are." They also needed to fill in four items for each of the other two courses.

"I think Dieter's Delight is salad, and Annoying Dripper is salad dressing." Jakob ran a finger down the menu. "Puddle Muddle sounds wet, so I'll order that and hope it's a drink. Fire Starter might be important for the beginning of the meal. I'll get that."

All around the room, people were guessing. Sarah listened in on other conversations, hoping for some clues as to what to order, but everyone else seemed as confused as they were.

"Single Dipper sounds like ice cream," Jakob decided, "so I'll save that for dessert. And Soapy Suds sounds like we have to do dishes. I'll stay away from that one."

"And I don't want the Root Canal. That sounds painful."

After everyone had ten minutes of discussion, one of the waiters rang a bell. "We'll be coming around to collect your orders now. No changes are allowed, and you have to eat everything you're served before the next course begins. No exceptions."

Sarah couldn't decide so she inserted random numbers in the blank spots. "I'll definitely be surprised."

Chuckles erupted around the room as the first course was brought in. Jakob's Puddle Muddle turned out to be gravy. To eat it, he had a Fire Starter (toothpick). He'd guessed right about the salad, but rather than dressing, he got water. Both he and Sarah had hoped High Rise would be silverware, but it turned out to be a yeast roll.

Sarah giggled as Jakob dragged his roll through the

gravy and ate his salad with a toothpick. One of her random numbers turned out to be a fork (Decision Points), so she was one of the few who ate her first course with silverware. Some people had ice cream and gravy for their appetizers.

By the time they reached the final course, they were laughing so hard they could barely eat. Jakob's only utensil for the first two courses had been the toothpick. Eating ice cream and mashed potatoes with a toothpick turned out to be challenging. By the time he reached the ice cream, it had melted, so he drank it from the dish.

Sarah's dessert consisted of chicken (Scaredy Cat), ice cream (Arctic Chill), mashed potatoes (Squishy Mortar), and a knife (Jam's helper). Sam had been expecting peanut butter (Jam's Helper), ice cream, and ginger snaps. Instead he received a knife, fork, and spoon (Single Dipper) to help him eat his Whipper Snappers (green beans).

By the end of the meal, everyone had figured out the list, but by then it was too late. And Jakob regretted not ordering the Soapy Suds because his favorite drink was root beer.

Squishy Mortar—mashed potatoes
Soapy Suds—foamy root beer
Jam's Helper—knife
Puddle Muddle—gravy
Crazy Mix-up—fruit salad
Annoying Dripper—water
Decision Points—fork
High Rise—yeast roll
Dieter's Delight—salad
Single Dipper—spoon
Whipper Snappers—green beans

Scaredy Cat—chicken
Root Canal—carrot boats
Arctic Chill—ice cream
Fire Starter—toothpick

After playing several other silly games, Jakob and Sarah were laughing so hard, they kept bumping into each other as they climbed the basement stairs. It seemed natural for him to take her hand the way he did when they were young, and he held it as they walked across the lawn to the buggy. Sarah reveled in their closeness, and although every nerve prickled, she reminded herself it was only friendship.

The whole way home, they laughed and chatted about their own and others' mishaps during dinner, and when they pulled into her driveway, Jakob asked if she wanted to go for a ride the next afternoon to catch the last of the fall color.

"I'd love to, but *Dat* made plans for us to visit *Aenti* Ruth." Sarah hated turning him down and hoped he'd ask again.

He appeared to be as disappointed as she was, which made her feel a little better. "Maybe we could plan it for next Saturday," Sarah suggested. *Oh, wait*, that wouldn't work either. "I forgot. We'll be going to Upper Dauphin to visit my sisters for the weekend. Would the Saturday after that work?"

Jakob nodded. "I think most of the leaves will be gone by then, but I'm sure we can find something to do. I really enjoyed spending time with you tonight."

"I had a lot of fun too." She wasn't positive, but she thought the light in his eyes didn't seem like the kind of look a man would give a little sister or a friend. Sarah lowered her eyes to prevent him from seeing the love shining in hers, but excitement coursed through her. Was it possible Jakob might come to care for her the way she cared for him? She got out of the buggy filled with hope for the future.

Chapter Seventeen

Sarah hummed to herself when she woke the next morning. Last night had been so much fun, and she kept replaying the look in Jakob's eyes, growing more and more certain with each repetition that his feelings for her might be more than friendship. She hugged the thought to herself as she fixed breakfast.

"I have some concerns about traveling today," *Mammi* said, her voice a bit shaky.

Mamm turned to her, worry in her eyes, "Do you need us to take you to the clinic?"

"No, no, I'll be fine. I'd just feel better staying home today."

"If you're sure?" *Mamm* appeared unconvinced.

Sarah studied her grandmother. *Mammi* had seemed fine when she came into the kitchen this morning. Her appetite was good; she'd even eaten two helpings. Something else was bothering her. The way she'd glanced toward the kitchen door several times gave Sarah a clue. She caught *Mammi*'s eye and flicked her head in the direction of the *daadi haus*. *Mammi* responded with a barely perceptible nod. Were the men causing a problem?

If *Mammi* was worried about leaving them unsupervised, her grandmother shouldn't stay here alone with them. Sarah had been so preoccupied with her rocky relationship with Rebecca and the thrill of spending time with Jakob, she hadn't thought much about the two men, especially now that they were taking care of their own meals. She'd promised *Mammi* they'd figure out the mystery behind Herman and Paul, but she'd done nothing about that. Perhaps now was the time to start.

Sarah cleared her throat. "*Mammi* shouldn't stay here alone. I'll stay home. Someone needs to be here in case she has any problems."

Mammi shook her head. "I'll be fine on my own. You go with your family. Your *Aenti* Ruth loves to see you."

"I can stay here," *Mamm* said.

"You were looking forward to seeing the quilt *Aenti* Ruth is making for Emma." Sarah had to convince *Mamm* to go. "I don't mind staying here. I've been exhausted the past few weeks. Perhaps a nap would help." Although she might not get an opportunity to rest.

"That's true." *Mamm* studied her. "You have been drawn and pale. I thought that would lessen once the wedding was over, but it only seems to have gotten worse."

So *Mamm* did pay attention to her after all, but her comments were less than flattering. What she said was true, though. Sarah's concerns about Rebecca kept her awake at night and left her preoccupied during the day. She hoped she and Rebecca could work things out so she'd have one less drain on her energy. Keeping all these secrets was wearing.

Sarah sighed. "Much as I love visiting *Aenti* Ruth, I'd prefer to stay home today." *So I can keep an eye on Mammi. And the men.*

"All right," *Mamm* agreed, "but try to rest while we're gone."

Unsure whether she'd have time for that, Sarah stood and began clearing the table. By the time she'd finished the breakfast dishes, the family was gone.

Mammi still sat at the table, sipping a second cup of coffee.

"What's going on?" Sarah asked.

"I'm not sure, but I got the impression they intend to do something while we're gone. I'm sorry I mentioned that we were planning this visit."

"But what do you think they're going to do?"

Mammi set her cup down with a bang. "I don't know. I overheard Herman on the phone several times confirming today's date. I stayed here so they'd think we all left together. Now let's go over and surprise them." With a rueful smile, she added, "If I'm wrong, I made us both miss a lovely visit with Ruth."

"I'm sure you have good reasons for your suspicions." Her grandmother's wisdom included discerning people's hidden motives, so Sarah was confident that if *Mammi* felt something was wrong, it most likely was.

After *Mammi* rinsed out her cup, the two of them put on their coats and headed out the door. As they crossed the walkway to the *daadi haus*, a passing buggy slowed almost to a halt.

Jakob. Before she could wave, the buggy picked up speed, and the horse trotted off. *Ach*, no. She'd told him she was going away with her family today, and instead she'd stayed home. What if he thought she'd made up an excuse to avoid going for a ride with him? If only she could dash after him and explain. Distressed, Sarah stared after the disappearing buggy.

While Sarah stood frozen in place, *Mammi* reached the door. Sarah quickened her pace to catch up. She'd have to let Jakob know what happened. Yet what could she say? Telling him she'd stayed to take care of *Mammi* wouldn't work. He'd seen *Mammi* outside walking, and she couldn't reveal the truth.

Her grandmother held out a hand to stop Sarah. Putting a finger to her lips, *Mammi* eased open the storm door and motioned for Sarah to hold it. Then she twisted the doorknob a little at a time until she could inch the door open. Sarah pushed all thoughts of Jakob from her mind. She'd have to find a way to make things right, but for now she needed to concentrate on figuring out what these men were up to.

Following *Mammi*'s lead, Sarah tiptoed down the hall. Herman's voice demanded to speak to Eric. She and *Mammi* stopped and listened.

"Coast is clear," he said. "I waited half an hour to be sure they wouldn't come back for something they'd forgotten. But you'll need to hurry because I have no idea how long they'll be gone."

"Yes, yes. Whatever it takes."

Mammi's eyes widened, and she reached for Sarah's hand. The question in her eyes was the same one on Sarah's mind: Should they let him know they were here, or would it be better to stay hidden and see what he planned?

Before Sarah could decide, *Mammi* stiffened her back and stepped into the room. Because she was still gripping Sarah's hand, she dragged Sarah with her.

Herman shrank back as if he'd seen a ghost. His eyes wide, pupils dilated, he stared at them. Then he burst out in a belligerent tone, "What are you doing home? I thought you were going on a trip?"

Hands on hips, *Mammi* faced him. "And what were you planning just now while you thought we were away?"

"N-nothing. Just going to have some company over."

"And you needed to wait until we were gone to do that?"

"Yeah, well…" Herman ran a nervous finger under the neckline of his shirt. "They'd be pretty uncomfortable around you people. Not your kind, you understand."

"I understand all right," *Mammi* said. "You were taking advantage of our absence to do heaven-knows-what. I guess it's good we decided not to go with the rest of the family."

Herman's expression wavered between anxious and annoyed. Then head down, lower lip stuck out like a petulant little boy, Herman clicked on his phone. "Cancel today's plans. Something unexpected came up." He listened for a second. "Can't talk now. Will explain later, but it's a no-go."

"You don't have to cancel on our account."

At the fake sweetness of *Mammi*'s words, Herman clenched his teeth and hung up his phone. "Like I said, these wouldn't be your kind of people."

"Well, let's make one thing clear. When you're a guest in someone's house, it's polite to ask the host or hostess if you may have company."

The front door banged open, and Paul came down the hall, whistling. He stopped short in the doorway. "Thought you were headed off to see an aunt."

"Yes, we were, but I got a nudge from God to stay home."

"You think God speaks to you?" Herman sounded incredulous.

"He'd speak to you too, Mr. Melville, if you'd go down on your knees and confess."

"No, thank you." Herman's voice had a sarcastic edge. "I like my life just fine the way it is."

"Do you really?" *Mammi* challenged.

Herman evaded her eyes.

Perhaps God would use *Mammi*'s words to convict these men. Sarah said a silent prayer that the Lord would touch their hearts.

"We also need to know how long you'll be here. I'm sure your *doctor* gave you a recovery time." *Mammi* pinned Herman with an eagle-eyed glance that made him squirm.

"Dr. Sanders said six to eight weeks, but I think we can wrap things up, er, I mean, I'm healing pretty quickly. I should be able to be moved in about two weeks."

Two weeks? That meant she and *Mammi* would miss going to Emma's and Lydia's next weekend. And she might have to miss her day with Jakob. If he'd even speak to her again.

Chapter Eighteen

The next morning before school, Rebecca looked drawn and pale as she sat at the desk, staring off into space. Sarah put a hand on her shoulder, and Rebecca jumped.

"I'm so sorry," Sarah said. "I didn't mean to startle you."

Rebecca rubbed her forehead. "I've been trying to figure out what to do."

"On Saturday you mentioned a big problem. Want to talk about it now?" Sarah settled onto a chair beside Rebecca's desk.

"Yes, but—" She pointed to the battery-powered clock on the wall. "The scholars will be here soon."

They still had ten minutes, unless a child arrived early, so Rebecca's problem must be pretty thorny if it needed more time than that. "Perhaps at recess or after school?"

"I guess."

Rebecca's lackluster response worried Sarah. Usually her friend chattered rapidly, rarely pausing for breath when she recounted things that bothered her. Today it seemed she barely had enough energy to talk.

"Are you ill? Do you need to go home?" Sarah placed

a palm on Rebecca's forehead, checking for fever. If anything, Rebecca's forehead felt cool rather than warm.

Rebecca shook her head, dislodging Sarah's hand. "I'm not sick, at least not that kind of illness. I'm just upset about something that happened this weekend."

The first scholars entered, and Sarah took charge. "Rebecca isn't feeling well," she whispered, "so let's talk quietly and try not to give her any trouble today."

After one of the usual troublemakers heard the message, his eyes gleamed. Sarah shook her head at him, and he slumped in his seat. She wasn't sure why, but usually a gentle reprimand from her calmed him and many of the other lively students Rebecca found hard to manage. Maybe it was because Sarah had played with most of them after church or babysat them after school or on weekends. She was grateful they listened well, because some of the fourteen-year-old boys were taller than she was. They would be hard to handle if they decided to be disrespectful.

The day passed quickly, and Sarah had no time to talk to Rebecca. Rebecca punished Joseph Yoder for disrespect by keeping him inside during recess, so she sat at her desk keeping an eye on him while he did extra schoolwork. Sarah took the rest of the class outside. When the children came inside, Rebecca sat at her desk, shoulders slumped, head in her hands. She rallied when Sarah asked her what was wrong.

Sarah eyed her throughout the afternoon. Rebecca threw herself into teaching and seemed almost her usual self as she taught the lessons, but between groups or when students were reciting, she drifted off, her eyes distant and sad. Sarah had trouble keeping her own mind on the scholars she worked with and longed for the school day to end, so she could talk with her friend.

It was with great relief that Sarah finally herded everyone from the building at the end of the school day. Then she turned to Rebecca, "Would you like to walk home with me so we can talk? *Mamm* was planning to make shoofly pie today." Because that was Rebecca's favorite dessert, she hoped it would entice her friend to come for a visit and spill her problem. After they'd gathered their things and put on their cloaks, Rebecca took Sarah's arm for the trek through the fields.

"*Danke* for inviting me to your house," Rebecca said. "I'm so *ferhoodled*, I don't know where to start."

Sarah turned sympathetic eyes toward her.

Rebecca took a deep breath and then blew it out. "You know when Abner and I left your house on Saturday night?"

"Yes, I was very worried about you." She hadn't intended to cover for Rebecca and Abner slipping out on dates away from family supervision. "What if your parents or Jakob had come by to ask about you? What would I have said?"

"They don't feel the need to check up on me when I'm with you. And I told Jakob not to pick me up this time."

"You used the trust your family has in me to disobey them?" Sarah cringed at how accusatory the question sounded. She only meant to help her friend do the right thing, not condemn her.

Rebecca winced. "Please forgive me. That was not my intent. I planned to stay in your living room, but Abner—" Tears formed in her eyes. "That's what I wanted to talk to you about."

"You can tell me. I hope I didn't sound like I was judging you, because I'm not."

"I know. That's why you're such a wonderful *gut* friend." Rebecca squeezed her eyes shut for a second. "This is so hard to tell."

As they walked past the drying corn shocks in the fields, Sarah remained silent, waiting for her friend to compose herself enough to continue.

"I told you about the job interview, and I did go with Abner to be sure he kept the appointment." Rebecca's voice was thin and reedy, quite different from her usual robust, confident tone. "But I also wanted to be alone with him. I thought if he got the job—" she swallowed hard "—we could talk about our future. He's always saying he doesn't make enough money to buy a house or livestock." Rebecca stopped suddenly, her eyes brimming with tears.

When Sarah turned toward her, she averted her eyes. "I—we went to a barn. One where they were having a party. He said that's where the interview would be."

"And you believed him?"

"I wasn't sure, but it turned out it was true. I'll tell you more about the job later. Anyway, Abner was acting very strange, and he asked me to dance. I didn't want to, but he begged me to try. When I said I had no idea how, he put his arms around me and cuddled me close. We just swayed back and forth to the music. I know I shouldn't have done that."

Sarah reached out and clasped both of her friend's hands. "Oh, Rebecca."

Rebecca pulled her hands away and started walking rapidly down the row. Sarah followed, not sure what to say. They walked for a few yards before Rebecca slowed enough for Sarah to catch up.

"I—I didn't want to tell anyone this part. When we went outside to the wagon, all he wanted to do was kiss." She gulped, and a soft hiccuping sound came from her lips, as if she were choking back sobs. "I told him to stop. And he did. I made him take me home right away. I'm sorry I didn't come back to your house that night, but I couldn't face anyone."

"I understand." Sarah wished she had a way to comfort her distraught friend.

"I knew you would. I also know I can trust you never to tell anyone."

"Of course. Your secret's safe with me. But what about Abner?"

"I don't know." Rebecca turned haunted eyes in her direction. "He came to the house on Saturday night to take me to the Mystery Supper, but I had *Mamm* tell him I had a headache."

Sarah wished she'd known. Jakob had mentioned a possible fight with Abner, but Sarah had been having so much fun with Jakob, she hadn't given Rebecca a second thought.

"Then Abner came over yesterday afternoon and asked to talk to me. I can't avoid him forever, so I went into the living room. We usually sit together on the couch, if Jakob isn't around to peek into the room. But I made Abner sit on a chair across from me. He looked really hurt, and I felt awful."

"You did the right thing," Sarah assured her.

"I know, but Abner came to apologize. He said he regretted what he'd done. He told me he's so attracted to me, it's hard for him to wait until we're married. I feel that way sometimes too, and I forgave him. He promised not to ever do anything like that again."

"And you believe him?"

"Of course. Why shouldn't I?" Rebecca demanded.

"I didn't mean that you shouldn't. He repented and you forgave him. I just wondered if you trust him to keep his word."

"I'm not sure. I know he was really sorry. He also promised we'd never go back to the barn again. He felt terrible about taking me there."

"That's good."

"Yes, it is." The worry lines in Rebeca's face smoothed out. "Then he told me how much he loved me." She wrapped her arms around herself, and a dreamy look came into her eyes. "I know we shouldn't think about marriage—or even courting—until we're both baptized, but our relationship is different—and special."

Sarah was unsure whether to be happy or concerned for her friend. They'd almost reached the back door, when Rebecca clutched her arm.

"I forgot to tell you the worst part."

There was more? Sarah held her breath, waiting fearfully for the rest of Rebecca's story.

"It's about the job. It turned out that he had an interview with a TV scout who's looking for stars for a new Amish show they'll be filming. The scout liked him and wants him to meet with the show's producer. The scout didn't tell him where the producer was staying—it's a closely guarded secret—but Abner gave the scout his cell phone number to set up a meeting."

Scouts, filming crews, and secret missions? Clues clicked together in Sarah's head. She had a sinking feeling she knew exactly where the producer was hiding out.

Rebecca continued, "The scout asked me if I was interested too, but I said no. And I don't want Abner to do it either. He'd have to leave for New York soon and stay until they're done shooting—that's what he calls it when they're making a movie. It sounds more like they're planning to kill him."

They would be killing him, if not physically, at least spiritually. Sarah, her heart heavy, didn't want to burden her friend with the questions burning in her brain. Would Abner miss baptismal classes and not be able to join the church next year? Worse yet, what if he preferred acting and big-city life? Would he ever come back to Rebecca and the church?

As they neared the back door, Rebecca said, "I don't know what I'll do, but thank you for listening, Sarah. You're the best friend ever." Suddenly, she stopped and pointed toward the black car parked near the barn. "What's Abner doing here?"

Sarah's stomach twisted. If she'd needed any more confirmation that her hunch was right, she now had it. Abner was here to meet the producer, but how could she explain that to Rebecca? Or the rest of the community?

Rebecca yanked open the back door and raced through the kitchen and down the hall to the living room, ignoring Sarah's calls to wait. By the time Sarah caught up with her, Rebecca stood in the empty living room, staring around as if she might spot Abner hiding behind the couch or chair. "Where is he?"

"I think I know," Sarah said heavily. "If I'm right, I have a long story to tell you, but first I need to check with *Mammi*." And the *producer*.

"You think Abner's talking to your grandmother?"

Rebecca followed Sarah down the hall and into the kitchen. "I'll come with you."

"No, I'll need you to stay here." Sarah reached for the shoofly pie *Mamm* had left cooling on the counter. "Why don't I cut you a piece? You can eat it while I talk to *Mammi*."

Rebecca crossed her arms, her jaw locked in determination. "I'll have a piece after we find Abner."

"Please, Rebecca? Just give me a little time alone with *Mammi*, and then I'll explain. And if Abner's there, I'll send him out here."

"I guess." Rebecca sank onto a bench at the kitchen table, a sulky expression on her face, which softened a little when Sarah set the pie in front of her and handed her a plate, knife, and fork.

"Just be sure to leave some of the pie. I think *Mamm* is planning to serve it for dessert tonight."

"Oh, you," Rebecca said, waving the fork at her. "I'm not that much of a pig that I'd eat it all."

"Right. You'll only gobble down half."

"Sarahhhh."

"I'm teasing, but be sure to count how many people will be eating dinner here tonight and save enough slices."

Leaving Rebecca contentedly munching a generous slice of shoofly pie, Sarah marched out the door and over to the *daadi haus* determined to get some answers.

Chapter Nineteen

This time when she opened the door, she didn't intend to give them any warning, although the door slamming behind her as she stalked down the hall might have alerted them. Conversation stopped, and *Mammi* peeked her head into the hall.

"Oh, it's you, Sarah." She beckoned her into the living room. "There's something you need to hear."

"I suspect I already know."

She stormed past her grandmother and into the living room. Spying her, Abner shrank into the corner. She'd deal with him later. First, she had something to say to Herman.

Hands on hips, she whirled toward the bed. "You lied to us."

"Whoa, now, hold on there, girlie. I didn't lie."

"All that talk about men killing you was so I'd feel sorry for you and let you stay here."

"That's not exactly what I said."

"No, you said you'd be *toast* and did this." She made a slashing motion across her neck.

"That's right. I'm sorry you misinterpreted my meaning."

"You did that deliberately. You wanted me to mis-understand."

"Perhaps a little, but you don't understand. This is a cutthroat business."

"Someone would actually kill you over a TV show?"

"Not physically, darlin'. But if they stole my idea before I had a chance to pitch it, I'd be history. In this business, that's death."

"You also lied about your leg. Kyle says you have a walking cast."

"So that sneak was trying to see my cast. I figured he was, but Paul told me I was imagining things."

When she continued to glare at him, he shrugged. "OK, maybe I fudged a bit about the leg."

"A bit? Is your leg even broken?"

Herman had the grace to look sheepish. "Only a badly twisted ankle, but it hurt as much as a broken bone."

"I'm sure it did." Sarah couldn't keep the sarcasm from her words. "So what changed that you don't have to keep everything secret? Or are you still trying to keep your plans secret from us while you go around trying to recruit people to be in your show?"

Herman threw his arms wide. "No need for secrecy anymore. We got the green light for the pilot, so we can start casting for the first episodes."

Green light. She'd heard him use those words the other day while he was talking on the phone. "I assume a green light means you can go ahead with your plans?"

"Sure does, darlin'. We can announce it to the world."

Sarah struggled to make sense of this. "First you're telling me people will kill you if they find out you're here. Now you intend to let everyone know? That makes no sense."

"You don't understand." Abner stood and puffed out

his chest. "All the other producers chase him and spy on him to find out what he'll do next because he's Hollywood's golden boy. He's super famous for his string of ten hit TV shows in a row."

Sarah wasn't certain what a golden boy was, but people didn't kill over TV shows. Before she could comment, Abner rambled on.

"Everyone's after his ideas. They follow him around, trying to figure out what he's planning. Then they try to scoop him."

Trying to decipher Abner's meaning was like struggling to understand someone who spoke a foreign language. Sarah stared at him, attempting to piece it all together.

"That's why he parachuted into the area a few weeks ago," Paul explained. "He didn't want anyone to know his latest ideas. We let him out in the Lancaster area, but the plane landed near Harrisburg, and other producers started speculating about his plans in the state capital. It threw everyone off our trail."

Herman snorted. "While they were busy nosing around there, trying to figure out my next moves, I put everything in place here for some great new shows."

Abner stared at Herman with admiration shining in his eyes. Then he turned toward Sarah. "Isn't it great how he fooled them all? The first show will have a secret peek into real Amish life. It won't be one of those fake staged shows."

How did Abner know so much about Herman and his plans? Then what Abner had said sank in. "He's the one who sent cameramen to Emma's wedding, isn't he?"

"He only wanted some footage for the show."

"Abner, surely you don't think that was acceptable?" Sarah's voice rose, and she tried to calm herself. "No one will let Herman film their life for a TV show."

"Don't be too sure about that," Abner muttered.

Sarah prayed she'd misheard. If she hadn't, her best friend might be headed for heartbreak.

Then she turned to Herman. "So you sneaked into our house under false pretenses and then set out to destroy our community?"

"First off, I didn't sneak in here. You invited me. And I have no intention of hurting your community. I'll bring you some fame and fortune. Put you on the map, so to speak."

"We don't want fame and fortune. We value…"

Her voice trailed off, and deep sadness enveloped her. She'd been about to say that they valued peace, kindness, and charity. And most importantly, following God's will. Yet she'd just spent all this time attacking him, insulting him. What kind of example was she of God's love? Herman hadn't intended to hurt them; he just didn't understand their ways. He assumed they'd be happy with what made him happy. And with her temper just now, what had she shown him about humility and forgiveness?

"I'm sorry I've been such a poor example of what our community values. I shouldn't have attacked you like that. We aren't interested in money and prestige, we value the things of the spirit—love, compassion, giving, and following God's commands. Will you forgive me for my sharp tongue?"

Herman waved a hand in the air. "Nothing to forgive. I enjoy sparring, and it was nice to see a little spunk out of you. Most of the time you're too nicey-nice."

Sarah wondered if it was possible to be too nice. *Mammi* smiled at her. Her grandmother had been silent all this time. Why hadn't she interfered to stop the rants?

"Sarah?" Rebecca called. "You were taking so long, I came to make sure everything was all right." She poked her head around the doorway, and her mouth dropped open when she spotted Herman sitting in the hospital bed. "What's going on?"

Her gaze flicked from Herman to Sarah and then back again. "You've been taking care of a sick person and never mentioned it to me?"

Sarah closed her eyes. How would she ever explain this situation? "Rebecca…"

But her friend's exclamation startled her. "You!"

Sarah opened her eyes to see Rebecca staring at Paul.

"Well, hello, again, doll." Paul's smile was warm and welcoming. "You change your mind?"

"I most certainly did not!" Rebecca whirled to face Sarah, her eyes wide. "What are these people doing in your house?"

"That's what I'm trying to figure out," Sarah said, a bit dazed. If Herman no longer needed to keep his plans secret, he also didn't need to stay here. That would be a relief. Then she remembered *Mammi*'s words about being a blessing. She prayed God would give them an opportunity to show His love.

In the far corner of the room, Abner hunched over as if trying to make himself smaller, less visible, but his movements drew Rebecca's attention. She turned to the right. "Abner?"

All the color drained from his face. "Rebecca, I can explain."

"He certainly can." Herman's hearty voice cut through the tension. "Meet the newest star of our TV show. Abner here is just about to sign on the dotted line."

Chapter Twenty

By the time Sarah got Rebecca calmed down and on her way home and Abner sent off with a warning to pray before signing the agreement, it was dinnertime. But Herman had one more bombshell.

He turned to *Mammi*. "I had another brainstorm." Herman studied her closely. "Yep, you'll be perfect. You have the right personality, biting wit, and chutzpah."

Paul laughed. "It may be a brilliant idea, but I doubt you'll get her to cooperate."

"Cooperate with what?" *Mammi* demanded.

"I can see it now." Herman drew his hands out in front of him in a huge rectangular shape. "I even know the font we'll use—it'll look like a cross-stitch sampler. *Homespun Wisdom*, doesn't that sound great?"

Mammi stood, a center of calm amidst Herman's growing exuberance as he sketched the outline for his latest idea.

"At first we'll just use it as a teaser to introduce the other show, but later it'll take on a life of its own. You like helping people, don't you? Giving advice?"

Arms crossed, *Mammi* stared him down. "It depends."

"You can put people in their places, threaten to wash their mouths out with lye soap, things like that. All the stuff you're so good at it."

Mammi only stared at him.

"I'll make you a star. In a few months, you'll be a household name. People will be tuning in from around the globe to watch your witty answers to life questions. Of course, you'll have to tone down the God-stuff. That won't fly with some of the viewers."

"I guess you didn't listen very closely to what my granddaughter said earlier. Our only purpose in life is to live a life that honors God."

"And you don't think helping millions of people have better lives would honor God? I'm sure it would make Him happy."

"What would make Him happiest, Mr. Melville, is for you to turn your life over to Him and live a godly life."

"See, comebacks like that are exactly what we're looking for. Snappy and unexpected jabs." Herman rubbed his hands together. "Perfect. Just perfect."

"That was not a comeback." *Mammi* emphasized each word. "It was an important truth for you to consider. And I do hope you'll consider it before it's too late." She turned to Paul. "And you too."

A sickish expression spread across Paul's face. "You sound like my grandmother. She was always telling me to repent so I could go to heaven."

"She sounds like a wise woman." *Mammi* shook a finger at him. "You should listen to her advice."

Paul swallowed hard. "Maybe I will."

Herman glared at him. "Don't you go getting soft on me, Paul."

Mammi whipped her head around and wagged her

finger at him instead. "You leave Paul alone. He's doing some important work in his life. Work you should do as well."

Herman waved away her words. "So whadda you say? The dress, the apron, all natural with no makeup. A little old gramma vibe with snarky sayings. I can make this huge, and I mean huge." He closed his eyes, an ecstatic look on his face. Then he opened them and faced *Mammi*. "You in?"

"I'll make you a deal, Mr. Melville," *Mammi* said, her words slow and measured. "If you promise to spend time thinking about your deepest core values—the truly important ones—and seriously and prayerfully consider God's call in your life, I promise to spend time thinking about your show."

"Really, you will?" Herman clasped his hands together, and his lips curved into a wide smile.

"You'll find me a woman of my word."

"Whoo-hoo!" Herman shouted.

"Remember the agreement, young man. I said 'seriously consider.'"

"Yeah, yeah. I know. But this is so awesome. Paul, did you charge my phone?"

Paul nodded and unplugged the cell phone from a box next to him. "All set."

"I'll get the ball rolling on this one. Everyone's going to love it!"

"And I'll be praying for you." *Mammi* spun toward the door. "We'll be late for dinner, Sarah. We'd better hurry."

The minute they were outside, Sarah turned to *Mammi*. "I can't believe you agreed to think about being on TV."

"With the deal I just made, the subject will never come up."

"How can you be sure when Herman's so determined?"

"He has two options. If he doesn't keep his end of the bargain, I don't need to keep mine. But if he does follow through and prayerfully considers God's will, do you really think he'll try to talk me into being on a TV show?"

"You may be right, *Mammi*. I hope you are."

"If I'm wrong, I'll keep my end of the bargain. I promised to seriously consider it, and I already have. I won't go against the *Ordnung* or God's will for my life."

Although Sarah smiled at her grandmother's cleverness, she wondered if it was wrong to mislead Herman that way. The best scenario would be if he turned his life over to God. Paul, at least, appeared to be thinking about it. Perhaps that was why God had brought them here.

Just before they entered the house, Sarah stopped. "I've been feeling so guilty about keeping this a secret. Now that we know what those men have been doing, we need to tell *Mamm* and *Dat* the truth before anyone else in the community finds out."

"A wise idea," *Mammi* agreed.

Sarah's hand trembled as she turned the knob. What would her parents say?

They walked into the steamy kitchen, where *Mamm* was fixing pot pie.

"Oh, good, Sarah, you're here. Can you set the table? Dinner's almost ready."

Sarah got out the plates. "Sorry I'm so late. Do you need any help?"

"No, just slice and butter the bread."

By the time Sarah finished, *Dat* and the boys had washed up after milking. Everyone gathered around the table and bowed their heads.

After they'd all said their silent prayer, Sarah took a deep breath. "*Mamm*, *Dat*, there's something I need to tell you." She explained about the parachute, finding Herman, and hiding him in the *daadi haus*. At her parents' shocked looks, she rushed on to describe what they'd discovered about the men since. Her brothers shot her surprised looks but continued to shovel in their meals. Sarah left out the part about *Mammi* being asked to star in a TV show. That was for her grandmother to tell.

Mamm stabbed her fork into a pot pie noodle with more force than necessary, but she didn't lift it to her lips. "You kept it a secret from us all this time?"

"I thought it was a matter of life and death."

Mamm shook her head. "Even so, you should have told us."

"Everyone was busy with Emma's wedding and..." Sarah didn't go on. Making excuses didn't justify her behavior. "I'm sorry."

Dat set down his milk glass. "I have no right to criticize anyone for keeping secrets after the one I hid for years, but inviting someone to stay in the house should be my decision."

"I know, *Dat*." Sarah hung her head. "I asked *Mammi*, but I should have asked you as well."

"This was something we needed to decide together as a family," *Dat* stressed. "And now that we know their true purpose, we cannot condone what these men are doing. Letting them stay here will send a message to the community that we support their endeavors."

Mamm nodded. "That's so."

"You'll need to ask them to either discontinue their activities or leave."

Sarah doubted she'd convince them to give up their activities, and she had no idea how she'd get them to leave, but she said, "Yes, *Dat*."

Dat stroked his beard. "It's too late today for them to find somewhere else to stay, but it needs to be done tomorrow."

Sarah wished *Mammi* could do it for her, but she'd gotten the family into this mess, so it was her responsibility to get them out of it. Tomorrow afternoon *Mamm* and *Mammi* would be at their monthly quilting circle, so she'd do it before they returned. *Lord, give me the courage and the words to say.*

The next day after school, she plodded to the *daadi haus*, fearful of Herman's reaction. She opened the door slowly, dreading each step of her walk down the hall and then saying the words she'd need to say.

Herman's voice carried down the hall. Evidently, he hadn't heard her come in. "Yeah, that's what I said, *Bonnet Rippers*, not *Bodice Rippers*. Same idea, only this'll be Amish girls." He laughed. "The kid's on board for the first episode. Name's Abner."

Sarah froze. Abner had signed that agreement?

"I agree. Abner's not the best name. We'll let marketing come up with a dreamy name to match his looks. Girls are going to tune in every week just to stare at him."

Her legs weak, Sarah leaned against the wall. Did Abner realize what they had planned for him? She had to find a way to let him know, talk him out of it.

"Unfortunately," Herman continued, "his girlfriend's not willing to cooperate, but we found a way around that."

What had they done to Rebecca? Sarah shouldn't be eavesdropping, but she had to protect her friend.

"So this Abner let Paul wire him for sound, and we sat across the parking lot and filmed him and his girl. Told him it was a screen test, but it went so well, it's already been approved as a segment of the first episode. First we filmed them dancing—nice and awkward, very realistic, and a great lead-in to the passionate kissing in the buggy."

Sarah closed her eyes. They'd been filming him and Rebecca, and Abner knew it. He'd agreed.

"The girl did great. When Abner didn't let up on the kissing, she went ballistic. It was awesome. Demanded he take her home and all. Couldn't have staged it better."

Nausea slid up Sarah's throat, filled her mouth with a bitter taste. She swallowed, but it burned her gut. Everything Abner had done with Rebecca had been fake. Scripted for the TV show. A show Rebecca had no idea she was on.

Sarah had promised *Dat* she'd ask the men to leave today, but she had to warn Rebecca. Now. She slipped out of the *daadi haus* and ran into Paul.

"Whoa." He put out his hands to steady her, but she yanked her arms away as if his touch scalded her. It did. He'd betrayed them. She'd believed him when he pretended to think about giving his life to God.

"What's the matter? You look upset. Did Herman do something—?"

Herman had done something all right and so had Paul, but she had to tell Rebecca, talk to Abner. Warn Rebecca not to go out with Abner because they'd be taped.

She broke away from Paul and raced to the barn. She hitched up the wagon so she could get to Rebecca's quickly. The whole ride she berated herself for allowing those men to stay, for believing Herman's lies, for allowing compassion to blind her to reality. Kyle had tried to warn her, and he was right.

When she rapped at the Zooks' front door, Jakob answered. She'd been so focused on talking to Rebecca, she hadn't planned what she'd say if someone else answered the door. She stood there, staring at him, her mind a blank.

"Is everything all right?" Jakob asked. "You look upset."

No, everything was all wrong, and she was to blame. She focused on her mission: tell Rebecca. "Is your sister here?"

"No, she and *Mamm* went to take a casserole to Susanna Rupp, who just had a baby."

"Oh, no." She couldn't talk to Rebecca at the Rupps' house.

"What's wrong? Do you want to come in?" His eyes seemed to beg her to stay.

Sarah broke eye contact before she forgot why she'd come. "No, no, I need to talk to Rebecca." Sarah couldn't tell him about Rebecca sneaking out to meet Abner, or about Rebecca and Abner's time at the barn, or about Herman taping Rebecca and Abner. Those were Rebecca's secrets.

Jakob pulled the door open wider. "You could wait here for her."

As much as she'd love to, the panic driving her wouldn't allow her to sit still. "I'd better go." She had to find Rebecca now.

"I see." The stiffness in Jakob's back and voice revealed she'd hurt his feelings, but if Rebecca and Abner had a date tonight, Paul might be planning to tape it.

"It's not that I don't want to spend time with you," she rushed to explain, "but it's urgent I speak to Rebecca."

"I'd be happy to give her a message."

"Oh, no, no." That wouldn't do at all. "I mean, it's private." That sounded unkind. "Thank you for offering, but it's something I need to tell Rebecca directly, discuss with her."

"Rebecca mentioned stopping by your house later. Perhaps you could talk to her then."

Sarah feared "stopping by her house" meant another date with Abner. She couldn't believe her friend would try that ruse again, especially after Sarah had made it clear the two of them couldn't meet at her house again. "I have to go," she said.

"Look, Sarah, if you don't want to spend time with me, just say so. I thought we had a good time at the Mystery Supper. But then yesterday I saw you…"

"Yes, I'm sorry. I need to explain about that, but first it's urgent I find Rebecca."

"And now, you can't get away from me fast enough."

"I'm not avoiding you." She turned and hurried to the wagon, calling over her shoulder, "I like spending time with you." Her cheeks heated. That sounded too bold, too forward. Why could she never seem to get things right when she was around Jakob?

The sadness in his eyes stayed with her long after the door closed, and his expression haunted her as she turned the horse toward the Rupp's house. She had to make things right with Jakob, but right now warning Rebecca was her first priority.

Chapter Twenty-One

"Sarah?" Ada Rupp's surprised expression quickly changed into a welcoming smile. "I expect you're here to see the baby."

"Actually I was looking for Rebecca."

"I see."

Ada's downcast expression made Sarah feel even guiltier. First Jakob, now Ada. She'd hurt two people in her rush to tell Rebecca. As long as Rebecca was here, she wasn't with Abner or being filmed, so Sarah could spend time being friendly.

Taking a deep breath to calm her jittery nerves, Sarah said, "My message for Rebecca can wait. Is it all right to see the baby?"

"Of course. Come in." Ada led her into the house where her five younger siblings sat on the kitchen floor, playing marbles. A toddler in a high chair babbled and held up her arms as Ada passed.

Ada patted her head. "I'll be right back. I'm taking my friend Sarah to see the new baby."

The way she emphasized the words *my friend* made Sarah feel guilty. She and Rebecca had been so close they hadn't paid much attention to the other girls near their age. Ada must be lonely for company if a casual visit meant so much to her. It couldn't be easy to care for six—now seven—younger siblings. Sarah gave Ada an extra warm smile as she opened the bedroom door.

Mary Zook sat close to the bed, talking in a quiet voice to Ada's *mamm*. Rebecca glanced up, and her eyebrows rose. Although she didn't say it aloud, Sarah could read the question in Rebecca's eyes: *What are you doing here?*

Mary Zook brushed off her half apron. "We'll be going so you can spend more time with your new company." She rose, and Rebecca stood with her.

"Wait." Sarah cringed inside at the bossiness of her tone and tried to make her next words less abrasive. "If Rebecca would like to stay longer, I'd be happy to drive her home."

"I don't know…" Mary Zook began.

"Please," she begged, earning her an exasperated look from Rebecca.

She'd added two more people to the list of those she'd hurt. First Jakob, then Ada. Now she'd forced Rebecca into an awkward position.

Rebecca heaved a barely noticeable sigh, but Sarah, who knew her friend's every mood, caught it. It added to her guilt, but she had to speak to Rebecca.

Mary Zook still appeared undecided, but then she shrugged. "No more late nights, girls." She turned to Sarah. "I want her home at an early hour."

Sarah understood her concerns but longed to explain that she hadn't been the one who kept Rebecca out so late. She held her peace and was rewarded by Rebecca's relieved smile.

After Mary left, Ada beckoned for Sarah to step closer to the cradle. "Meet David," she whispered.

Although she'd always adored babies, Sarah's nerves were so taut she barely glanced at the infant. Noticing the wounded look in Ada's eyes, she bent over the cradle and cooed over the baby. She shouldn't allow her own fears to overshadow the joy of a birth. She'd have time to talk to Rebecca later. She relaxed and smiled down at the little boy. Her brow wrinkled as she studied the almost translucent skin with its bluish cast. The baby jerked and startled himself awake. His thin, weak cry made Sarah worry about his health.

Ada lifted the crying baby and handed him to her mother. "I'll take my friends to the kitchen while you feed him."

Her *mamm*'s wan smile didn't reach her eyes. "Thank you for coming, girls. And do thank your mother for the casserole and cake, Rebecca. I know we'll all enjoy it."

With murmured congratulations, the girls exited the bedroom. As Ada closed the door, she remarked, "David has heart trouble." Then she turned to Rebecca. "I'm grateful Jakob is setting up a benefit auction for his operation." Then she strode ahead of them into the kitchen.

Of course, Jakob would volunteer to set up a fundraiser. He had such a big heart. Every day, Sarah fell more in love with him.

Rebecca sidled nearer to Sarah and, behind Ada's back, mouthed that she wanted to leave. Sarah nodded, but didn't want to injure Ada's feelings any more than she already had, so she mouthed back, *Soon.*

Ada pulled out a bench and motioned for them to sit. "People dropped off some cake, pies, and cookies. What would you prefer?"

"Cookies sound good to me," Sarah said.

As soon as Ada turned her back, Rebecca tipped her head in the direction of the door, and her jaw tightened. She made a motion as if to stand, and Sarah grabbed her arm.

"Please stay," Sarah mumbled, low enough so Ada couldn't hear.

A fight broke out among her siblings, so Ada plunked the cookie plate on the table and rushed over to pull apart two wrestling boys and calm a sobbing girl. With hugs and soothing words, she soon restored order and joined them at the table.

Sarah sent Ada an admiring glance. "It must be a lot of work helping with all the little ones."

"*Jah*, some days it is, but I'm grateful for the experience. When I have children of my own, I'll know how to care for them."

So many of Sarah's friends had heavy responsibilities overseeing younger brothers and sisters. Having older sisters meant Sarah had few childcare duties. And Rebecca was the youngest in her family, so she'd always been the center of attention. With an older brother like Jakob to coddle and protect her, she'd grown up expecting others to care for her. Maybe Rebecca was drawn to Abner because he needed her help.

"Sarah?" Ada held out the plate of cookies.

"I'm sorry." Sarah took two sugar cookies and passed the plate to Rebecca, who took one, but begged Sarah with her eyes to leave.

Ada sat near Mary Elizabeth and finished feeding her with one hand, while she ate her cookie with the other and described the baby quilts she was making for an *Englisch* craft shop. "I can stay home and help

Mamm, but still earn money. So far they've been selling well. The *Englischers* who visit Lancaster County buy them."

"That's wonderful," Sarah said, and Ada's shy smile showed she appreciated the interest and attention.

As soon as they finished the cookies and the glasses of root beer, Sarah stood. "*Danke* for the food and for having us, but we really should get going. I promised Rebecca's *mamm* I'd get her home early."

After the door shut behind them, Rebecca burst out, "I thought we were never going to get out of there. What were you thinking accepting her offer of a snack?"

"I was thinking," Sarah said patiently, "that Ada looked lonely and needed some friends, even if only for a short time."

"I guess." Rebecca's response contained an edge of resentment.

Sarah stopped walking and stared at her. "This isn't like you." Her usually sweet-natured friend had become so prickly that Sarah hardly recognized her.

Rebecca avoided her eyes. "Let's go," she said brusquely.

They climbed into the wagon, and when Sarah flicked the reins, the horse trotted off. Now that she had Rebecca here with her, though, she was tongue-tied. She drove in silence a few minutes, struggling to find the words.

Finally, she turned to Rebecca and forced herself to start. "I have something terrible to discuss with you. That's why I came to Ada's."

"Is someone hurt? Somebody died? Why didn't you just tell me in front of my *mamm*?" Rebecca demanded.

Then her eyes widened, and she clutched Sarah's arm. "Did something happen to Abner?"

Sarah shook her head. "No, but what I have to say concerns him."

Rebecca crossed her arms and sat back with a sulky expression. "I don't want to hear it."

"You have to. Something awful has happened."

"But Abner's all right?"

"If you're referring to his health, as far as I know, he's perfectly fine." Sarah clucked to the horse and pulled on the reins to turn right before she spoke. "Do you remember seeing Abner with the producers?"

"If you're trying to make me upset, it's not going to work." Impatience in her voice, Rebecca said, "You convinced him not to sign the contract, remember? So let's not dwell on the past."

"Unfortunately, what I have to say refers to the future—yours and Abner's." Sarah cut off Rebecca's protest and plowed on. "Abner may not have signed that contract, but he did make an agreement with the producer."

"Sarah, why are you doing this? We were both there. I saw what happened. He made no such agreement."

"What about that night at the barn?"

Rebecca started to say something, but then pressed her lips into a mutinous line.

A car roared up behind them, revving its engine. Sarah pulled onto the shoulder to allow it to pass. "What did Abner say about the interview, Rebecca?"

"He said they'd offered him a job. He obviously didn't take it if he never signed the contract."

Her friend's *so-there* tone cut Sarah deeply. Rebecca sounded so angry and frustrated with her, and she hadn't even gotten to the worst part. How would Rebecca take it when she knew the truth?

Sarah checked for traffic behind her before encouraging the horse back onto the road. "Abner agreed to do a screen test."

"So what? The important thing is that he didn't."

"Yes, he did do one, and so did you."

"Sarah Esh, stop the wagon this instant. I'll walk home from here. I may have done some things I'm ashamed of—I've confessed most of them to you—but if you don't know me well enough to know I'd never do something like that..."

Holding up a hand, Sarah halted the flow of Rebecca's words, but she couldn't stop the anger pulsing from Rebecca. "Just hear me out. I didn't say you agreed to do a screen test. I said you did one." Before Rebecca could interrupt, Sarah pulled the horse into a graveled turnaround, turned to face her friend, and poured out the whole story.

"I don't believe you. Abner would never do something like that. Never." Rebecca's voice quavered. "I thought you were my friend. How could you make up such awful lies?" Tears pooled in her eyes.

"Rebecca, why would I lie to you?"

"To get me to break up with Abner, the way my family—and Jakob—want me to. I thought you were on my side. Instead you've teamed up with my brother."

"There are no sides here. My only concern is your well-being."

"And how much influence did my brother have on you that you'd concoct such ridiculous lies and expect me to believe them?"

"I'm not lying. I've only ever been truthful with you."

"Oh, really? Did you tell me about the producers you were hiding at your house? Did you tell me you were dating my brother?"

Now it was Sarah's turn to hang her head. "No." She yearned to defend herself, explain why she kept the producers a secret. Tell Rebecca she and Jakob were only friends. But it would only sidetrack the conversation and prevent Rebecca from facing the truth.

"Well, at least you're honest about that," Rebecca said grudgingly, when Sarah sat, head bowed.

And what if I've been honest about this as well? What then, Rebecca?

Chapter Twenty-Two

Silence stretched between them. Her head still bowed, Sarah closed her eyes and prayed silently that God would open her friend's heart and allow her to accept the truth. When she opened them again, tears were trickling down Rebecca's cheeks.

"Who told you this, Sarah?"

Sarah flushed. "I overheard Herman talking on the phone." Her stomach churned again as it had then.

"You were eavesdropping?"

"I didn't mean to at first, but when I heard him mention Abner's name, I stood there and listened. So, yes, I was eavesdropping."

"Maybe you misheard?" Rebecca used her sleeve to wipe the tears.

"I wish I had, but Herman's voice was loud and clear."

Rebecca took a shaky breath. "Abner was acting out of character that night. I thought it was nerves, but…" She closed her eyes, her face screwed up in pain. "I have to talk to him. I have to know if it's true… Maybe Herman lied."

Sarah hadn't thought of that possibility. Herman did have a tendency to stretch the truth or lie outright when it suited his purposes.

"I'm going to call Abner now." Rebecca opened her satchel and pulled out her phone.

Sarah tuned out her friend's tearful conversation. She had eavesdropped on Herman, but she wouldn't do it to Rebecca.

After she hung up, Rebecca's whole body slumped. "I trusted him. I can't believe he betrayed me like that. What am I going to do?" she wailed. "If the show's on TV, someone will see it and tell Jakob or *Mamm* and *Dat*."

Rebecca helped out in the family's woodworking business in the summer and on Saturdays, taking orders and delivering the smaller items. They did business with so many *Englischers*, no doubt one of them would recognize her on TV and mention it to the family.

Rebecca gulped. "I wanted to put that night behind me, forget all about it. Instead, the whole world will know." She covered her face with her hands. "It's like the Scripture says, 'Be sure your sin will find you out.'"

"Oh, Rebecca, I'm so sorry this happened. I feel like it's all my fault for letting Herman stay at my house, for not trying to find out what they were doing."

"That's true, but you had nothing to do with me sneaking out, going to the party, and all the rest. If I hadn't been there, they'd never have filmed me." She sat, her hands gripping the seat of the wagon so hard, her knuckles turned white. "I have to tell *Dat* and *Mamm* before they find out from someone else. Will you go with me?"

"This is between you and your parents. I don't think—"

"I can't do it alone. Please, Sarah?"

Sarah couldn't refuse; besides, she owed Rebecca's parents an apology for harboring the producer in the first place. And now that Rebecca planned to confess, Sarah could explain this afternoon's behavior to Jakob.

With a flick of the reins, Sarah started the wagon. The horse plodded along, but she couldn't bring herself to speed up the pace because of her reluctance to face Jakob and his parents. She'd always admired Jakob's honesty. Even when they were young, he never told a lie. She tried to copy his example while they were growing up, and until recently, she'd done her best to be scrupulously honest. Now she was enmeshed in such a tangle of deliberate omissions, half-truths, and outright lies, she often was no longer sure of what was truth.

The rest of the trip Sarah tried to frame an explanation for what had happened, but excuses only added to the burden she carried. Better to admit everything no matter how painful it was. But would telling the truth cost her Jakob's respect and destroy any chance of a relationship?

When they arrived at the Zooks', Rebecca remained in the wagon, and Sarah had to pry her friend's fingers loose from the wagon seat. As they made their way up the walk, Rebecca clung to Sarah's arm, dragging her to a halt before they reached the front door.

"I can't do this. I'm too ashamed to tell *Mamm* and *Dat*. I can't bear to see the disappointment on their faces."

"Let's both pray for courage to tell the truth." Sarah

bowed her head, and beside her Rebecca did the same. Then they made their way into the house.

They had missed dinner, but neither of them had an appetite, so they refused Mary's offer to reheat the casserole. Rebecca asked her *mamm* to meet with them in the bedroom so her *dat* could hear what she had to say. Mary Zook left the dishes, which Rebecca promised to wash later.

"Where's Jakob?" Rebecca asked.

"He went over to the Kings to meet several other young men. They're planning the benefit auction for the Rupp baby's heart operation. I expect he won't be back until late." Mary Zook settled in a chair beside the bed. "What is so urgent I need to leave the dishes undone, *dochder*?"

Rebecca hung her head. "I have a confession to make."

As the story tumbled out interspersed with tears, Hiriam and Mary Zook's expressions changed from angry to shocked and then to fearful. Rebecca described sneaking out to meet Abner, going to the barn, tasting alcohol, and kissing in the buggy.

"Oh, Rebecca," Mary Zook choked out. "I never thought…" She studied her daughter's face and then turned to Sarah.

"Sarah's not to blame," Rebecca said hastily.

"I didn't think she was. I only—"

"But I am to blame for what happened next." Sarah couldn't let Jakob's parents assume she was innocent.

Mary Zook pressed her clenched hands against her heart. "There's more?"

Although Hiriam Zook's features were slightly crooked and droopy on one side due to the second stroke he'd had recently, the disapproval on his face was clear. Like Jakob, he adhered to an extremely high standard. To hear his daughter admit to disobeying, lying, sneaking out, and attending parties must be a shock. And as for the kissing, Emma used to tease Lydia because Jakob had never kissed her, a fact that Sarah had always found strangely comforting. His father must have expected him to be chaste. He would expect the same of Rebecca.

"In many ways, this is the worst part for me, but perhaps it's fitting punishment," Rebecca said and then went on to tell about the filming.

Mary Zook closed her eyes and shook her head.

His speech painfully slow, Hiriam responded, "They...should...not...do...that...without...permission."

Rebecca's *dat* might be right, but Herman had no qualms about forging Sarah's name for the wedding filming. He could do it again.

Mary took his hand. "We'll have to see if there's anything we can do to stop it."

Now it was time for Sarah's confession. "What Rebecca hasn't told you is that I'm the one responsible for the producer being here."

Both the Zooks raised their eyebrows and stared at her.

"Although I didn't know who he was at first, I helped a man who got hurt." Sarah went through the story and added her recent discoveries. "He was also the one who sent the camera people to Emma's wedding."

When she responded, Mary's voice was gentle. "You were trying to be kind and help a stranger. You can't blame yourself for his actions."

"Except that *Mammi* and I both suspected something

was odd soon after he moved in. If I'd investigated the way I'd promised *Mammi* I would, none of this would have happened."

"Perhaps not," Mary said. "But it did occur, so we must accept that it's God's will."

"I'd still like to apologize. Will you forgive me for the trouble I caused your family?"

Mary's *yes* and the bishop's nod lifted one burden from Sarah's soul. Now the only one left to apologize to was Jakob. She hadn't meant to hurt him today or on Saturday.

Beside her, Rebecca was sobbing. "I told Sarah earlier she's not to blame. If I'd been obedient, the producer couldn't have filmed me."

"That's true, *dochder*."

"I'm so sorry, *Mamm* and *Dat*. Will you forgive me?"

After both her parents had extended their forgiveness, Mary asked, "And you will not do this again?"

"Oh, no, I promise. I'm not sure if I'll ever see Abner again." Rebecca hung her head. "And I know I'll need to be punished for my disobedience."

Mary looked at Hiriam, who was struggling to speak. "If…this…is…made…public…you…will…have…been… punished…enough."

"If you do decide to see Abner again, even if he wants to apologize, the only place you may meet him is in our living room, where one of us will be closely supervising you." Then Mary Zook turned her attention to Sarah. "If Rebecca asks about meeting Abner at your house, I hope you will say *no*."

"I will. In fact I already told her she could not invite Abner over again."

"Very good," Mary said with a smile. "I'm glad I can count on you to support our decision."

Although Sarah wanted to wait until Jakob came home, she could think of no excuse for doing so. "I need to be heading home now."

Rebecca's misty-eyed smile was filled with gratitude. "I'll walk you to the door." After Sarah said her good-byes to Rebecca's parents, her friend took her arm, and they headed into the living room. "Thank you for coming in with me. I wouldn't have had the courage to do that if you hadn't been here."

"I'm glad both of us were honest with your parents. It's such a relief not to be hiding the truth."

"And not to be taking your guilt out on your best friend," Rebecca admitted. "I'm sorry for being so grouchy and short-tempered with you when it was my-self I was angry with. Will you forgive me for that as well?"

"I've already forgiven you for that." Grateful that peace had been restored and they both had clean con-sciences, Sarah hugged her best friend.

Rebecca waved as Sarah got into the wagon, and Sarah waved back, her spirits lighter than they had been for quite a while. But the closer she got to home, the more nervous she became. She still had to confront Her-man and ask him to leave. *Lord, give me the courage and strength to do what needs to be done.*

It was dark by the time she got home, but a light still burned in the *daadi haus* living room. *Mammi* would be in bed by now, but the men were still up. She'd do it now.

She wasn't sure where to start first. Her indignation at Herman's treatment of Rebecca bubbled up inside, but if she started an argument over his actions, Herman might get upset and refuse to cooperate when she asked him to leave. She struggled to tamp down her fury each time she thought of the secret filming, and she banged through the front door and charged toward the living room without stopping.

"Whoa, somebody's in a temper," Herman remarked as Sarah barreled into the living room. He held his hands up as if they were a camera lens. "Angry girl enters stage left."

"Do you think of everything as scenes in movies?" Sarah demanded. "I don't imagine it allows you much time for actually living your life."

Herman laughed. "That's the fun in life."

"I find this hard to understand. Spending time setting up fake scenes is better than relating to real people?"

Herman blinked a few times as if he were struggling to understand.

Sarah continued, "Perhaps playing pretend is a cover-up for loneliness or a way to avoid facing the truth."

"Of course not," he blustered. Then he studied her. "What happened to that sweet, quiet girl I first met?"

Shame coursed through Sarah. She should be demonstrating God's love instead of criticizing and blaming.

"You know," Herman said, "your tongue is getting as sharp as your grandmother's. You were so gentle and nice when I first arrived."

And naïve, as Kyle had pointed out. Sarah wasn't sure this recent change was for the better, although if she ended up with *Mammi*'s wisdom, it might be a good thing.

"I'm sorry for losing my temper. Will you forgive me for criticizing you?"

"Huh?"

Paul spoke for the first time. "She's asking you to forgive her. Of course, you will, so the answer's *Yes, I forgive you.*"

Herman shook his head. "I'm not getting into all this religion stuff."

"You need to get over your hang-ups about religion, especially if you plan to do this series. Forgiveness is important to the Amish, isn't that right?" He turned to Sarah with a question in his eyes.

"That's true. We need to forgive others the way we want God to forgive us."

Herman held up a hand. "Enough with all the God stuff. So," he said to Sarah, "you came in here like a mother bear defending her cubs. And I think I know why. Paul said he ran into you outside and you were upset. My guess is you listened in on a private conversation."

Sarah's cheeks flamed, and she ducked her head. "I'm sorry."

"Stop with the apologizing already. It makes me nervous."

"Perhaps because you need to do a lot of it yourself," Paul teased.

"That's my own business," Herman growled.

"Yours and God's," Paul corrected.

Herman narrowed his eyes. "Since when did you start getting all religious?"

"Watching Sarah and hearing her *mammi*, I've decided I need to go back to my grandmother's teachings. So expect some big changes."

Herman grumbled under his breath.

Paul gestured toward Sarah. "We've gotten off track.

Judging from her expression, Sarah came rushing in here to say something important. So we should listen."

Now that Paul had turned their attention to her, Sarah's throat went dry. How could she tell them to leave in a polite way? She should have rehearsed this ahead of time, decided what to say.

Taking a deep breath, she plunged into *Dat*'s request. "Last night I told my parents about you being here, and they were fine with extending hospitality to those in need. But the truth is, you aren't in need."

"I need a place to stay," Herman said.

Paul crossed his arms. "One you could easily afford to pay for."

Sarah continued, "You were here under false pretenses. You led me to believe your leg was broken and you needed a place to stay because you'd be killed. Neither of those were true."

Paul directed a mocking smile Herman's way. "Sounds as if someone needs to apologize."

Herman only glared at him.

"But what upsets me most is that you hid your profession. Knowing that we don't believe in having our pictures taken, you proceeded to film parts of our private lives. I need to shoulder the blame for not investigating sooner, for not realizing what you were doing."

Herman drummed his fingers on his closed laptop. "And your point is?"

Sarah walked over to the bed. "I have two actually." She ticked them off on her fingers. "One, you took advantage of my family and friends and violated our beliefs when you filmed us. Two, my parents were extremely upset to learn about your profession. *Dat* is concerned that the community will think we condone what you've done if we allow you to stay here." Sarah took a deep breath. "He wants me to ask you to find another place to stay."

"You know," Herman said, "you're really cute when you're angry. Have you ever considered acting?"

Sarah stiffened. "Did you hear what I said about our beliefs?"

"Yeah, something about violating them, but I have a great idea. Let's try a screen test," Herman said, grabbing her arms and pulling her toward his puckered lips.

Behind her someone sucked in a breath. "Sarah!" The shock in Jakob's voice sliced through her.

Chapter Twenty-Three

She turned her head and met Jakob's eyes. She knew how it must look, her partially leaning over the bed, Herman's hands on her arms, him about to kiss her. She jerked her hands out of Herman's grasp.

"The storm door and front door were both open, so I worried something might have happened to you. I—I guess I should have knocked."

Herman laughed. "The perfect scene. Boyfriend shocked to find girlfriend in arms of a lover."

Jakob's face went a sickly white. "Lover?"

"Don't listen to him, Jakob. He's a liar."

His eyes sadder than she'd ever seen them, Jakob asked, "And how about you, Sarah? Have you ever lied to me?"

Sarah squeezed her eyes shut. How could she answer that? Several months ago, she could have met his eyes and in a clear, steady voice answered, "No, never." But now, she'd hidden so many things from so many people, sometimes she wasn't sure she even knew the truth any more.

"I thought we were starting to build a relationship."

The quiet finality of his words cut more deeply than anger or disgust. "One of the expectations I have for the woman I date is that she be completely honest."

The woman he dates? He'd been thinking of her in that light? If so, she'd just destroyed her dream.

With one last look that tore Sarah's soul to ribbons, Jakob spun on his heels and left the room.

"Touching, touching." Herman clapped. "Almost brought tears to my eyes. I'd be happy to sign both of you."

When Sarah whirled to face him, devastation and fury in her eyes, he held up his hands. "OK, so maybe not."

Sarah longed to run after Jakob, tell him everything, beg him to forgive her. But what could she say? How could she explain? With all the covering up she'd done, she'd never meet Jakob's standards. She saw her actions through his eyes. Hiding facts, omitting details, allowing others to think something that wasn't true—those were all forms of lying. Not something he'd accept in a relationship.

The woman he'd date. Each word was a lash to her heart. A reminder of how she'd failed.

Paul cleared his throat. "Sarah, I'm sorry. For everything. We've done damage here, mostly out of ignorance. Although I studied a bit about the Amish lifestyle, I didn't realize…" His voice raspy, he continued, "I had no idea our actions would impact your hopes and dreams and strong beliefs. And no idea of the devastation we'd cause. Can you forgive us?"

A tear trickled down Sarah's cheek. She'd lost Jakob, but God had brought some good out of the situation. He seemed to be working in Paul's heart.

Now Sarah struggled to let go of the problems and pain that Paul's and Herman's actions had caused—for herself, for Rebecca, for Abner, for all the guests at Emma's wedding. She bowed her head and whispered, *Dear Lord, please give me a forgiving heart.*

Then one by one, she turned each of her disappointments and distresses over to God. When she finally looked up, she could face Paul with an unburdened heart and a clear conscience. "Yes," she said. "I forgive you." And though it was harder to do, she faced Herman. "I forgive you too." As she uttered the words, the burdens she'd been carrying around for weeks rolled away.

"I didn't ask for it." Herman's gruff tone didn't match the softness in his eyes.

Paul's face brightened. "Don't let Herman fool you. We both appreciate it."

"Speak for yourself," Herman muttered.

After giving him a dirty look, Paul continued, "Now that's out of the way, we need to talk about us moving out. I'll find a place tomorrow, a hotel or something, until we can find a rental property. I'll need something with laundry service, though, because we've used up all the clean clothes in the duffle bag."

"I'd be happy to wash them for you."

"No, no," Paul said, "you've done enough already. And that reminds me. We did want to compensate you for staying here. I've felt guilty imposing on you without paying."

"We couldn't take anything."

"Nevertheless, I want to do it." He reached in his pocket, grabbed a thick stack of bills from his wallet, and fanned them out.

Sarah gasped. They were all hundred dollar bills.

Herman's sarcastic voice jolted her back to the room. "So, she's not as immune to money and worldly goods as she seems."

Paul ignored him. "Is $100 a night acceptable? And then several hundred for meals?"

Sarah put her hands behind her back. "Like I said, we can't take it."

Herman laughed. "What a good negotiator. You even look like you mean it. Trying for more, eh?"

"No, I'm not."

A loud knocking echoed through the room. "Sarah, may I come in again?" Jakob called. "I have something I need to say."

Sarah wasn't ready to hear more. What she'd heard earlier still stung, but she couldn't leave him standing there. "Come in," she called.

Paul added two more hundreds to the ones he'd already held out. "Is that better?"

"Like I said, I can't accept your money."

"You sure?"

"I'm positive. We took you in because it's what God would want us to do."

Paul was getting ready to return the money to his wallet when Jakob stepped into the room.

"Wait," Sarah said. "Would you give the money to him?"

Herman snickered. "You hoping paying off your boyfriend will make him forget what he witnessed earlier? Sweeten the pot a little?"

Jakob glared at him.

"Please, Paul?" Sarah said.

Paul shrugged. "It's all the same to me."

Jakob stared at the stack of bills Paul held out to him. "What's this?" He looked at Sarah in confusion.

"It's a donation for the Rupp baby's heart operation."

"It is?" Jakob asked, and Herman echoed the question.

"Jakob's been organizing a benefit auction for the baby. The parents can't afford to pay for an operation."

Herman looked suspicious. "Nice try, doll, you might get Paul to believe you, but I'm not that stupid. If it's a necessary operation, insurance will cover it. What do you really have planned for the money?"

"I don't think the Amish have insurance," Paul said.

"No, we don't believe in it," Jakob said.

"Don't believe in it? How crazy is that?"

"Herman…" Paul warned. Then he took out his wallet and added the three remaining hundreds in it to the wad he held out to Jakob.

"You're giving him all your money?" Herman screeched. "Talk about crazy!"

Paul gave him a look that quieted him.

Herman waved a hand in the air. "It's your money." His tone made it obvious he didn't approve.

"Yes, it is," Paul said. "And there's plenty more where that came from, isn't there, Herman? You could probably add to it."

"I don't think so." But under Paul's steady gaze, Herman pulled out his wallet and added two fifties and a hundred.

A dazed look on his face, Jakob took the money. "Thank you so much. This is an amazing start to the fund."

"That was extremely generous, so thank you," Sarah told both of them.

Herman cleared his throat loudly several times until he had everyone's attention, but then he directed his words to Jakob. "I'm not her lover."

"I know that. Sarah wouldn't…" Jakob looked chagrined.

Herman averted his eyes. "Yeah, well, I just thought you should know it wasn't true."

Sarah stared at him in amazement. Had Herman just admitted he'd lied? In a roundabout way, but still… Joy bubbles fizzed and popped inside. God must be working in his heart too.

Jakob caught Sarah's eye. "Actually I was upset about something else. That's what I came back to talk about if you have time, Sarah?"

"I have one more thing I need to discuss with them." Sarah gestured toward Paul and Herman.

Jakob held up a hand. "I apologize. I didn't mean to come in here and interrupt your conversation. We can talk some other time."

"This won't take long, and I'd like to talk to you. Maybe you could head over to the kitchen to wait. I'll be over shortly." This time she didn't ask if he knew the way to the kitchen.

"I'll do that," he said.

As soon as the front door closed behind him, Sarah rounded on Herman. "You've taken some unauthorized photos, and I want them destroyed. You had no right to take photos of Rebecca without her knowledge."

"Rebecca? Who's that?"

How many girls had he filmed? "Abner's girlfriend."

"Oh," Herman looked sickish. "That's some of my best work."

"Rebecca never signed a permission form."

"You mean a model release form?" Paul asked.

"Whatever it is that allows you to show her picture on TV. If her parents decided to take legal action…"

"Hey," Herman groused at Paul. "I thought you assured me these people don't believe in suing."

"They don't," Paul said. "I'm sure Sarah's only suggesting a hypothetical situation, aren't you?"

"I can't speak for Jakob's parents, but…" Sarah couldn't imagine the Zooks initiating a court case, but they'd want to protect Rebecca.

Herman clenched his jaw and pounded his fist on his laptop.

"Careful," Paul warned. "You don't want to damage that."

Pounding one fist into his open palm instead, Herman moaned. "I can't believe this. My best work ever. So real, so natural, so perfect." He glared at Sarah. "You not only cleaned out our wallets, now you want to destroy my livelihood."

"Oh, stop bellyaching," Paul told him. "You'll figure out something just as wonderful. You always do."

Grumbling under his breath, Herman rolled his eyes upward. A few seconds later, he shouted, "Give me my phone."

Paul handed him the cell and said to Sarah, "He always gets like this just before he has a brilliant idea. If he does, maybe your friend won't appear on the show."

Herman swiped and tapped on his phone. "We've run into some filming problems here. We'll be headed back, so start building a set and begin casting immediately. Use the segment I've sent as an example. We'll use that in lieu of a script."

Sarah wasn't positive she understood what he was

saying, but it sounded as if Herman planned to film Rebecca's scene using actors. She'd wait to confirm it when he got off the phone.

After he barked a series of additional commands into the phone, Herman hung up. "We won't need a hotel. Paul, get us flights back first thing tomorrow morning. Hire a private plane if you can't get first class."

"Will do." Paul grinned and said to Sarah, "I guess your friend and the rest of the community won't have to worry about being filmed."

"That's right." Herman's face twisted into a sour expression. "All that great footage lost."

"Look on the bright side," Paul said. "You can tell the actors what to do, and they'll have to do it. Real people are unpredictable."

"That's true, I suppose."

"You'll be in your element—barking out commands and people jumping to obey."

"You saying I'm bossy?"

"If the shoe fits..." Paul grinned. "So, Sarah, it looks like we'll be out of here permanently tomorrow morning."

A great sense of relief flooded through Sarah. God had handled this situation in a way that was better than she could have imagined.

"Don't be so sure about that," Herman retorted. "I'm still planning to do my *Homespun Wisdom* show. Remind your grandmother I'm counting on her."

"And she's counting on you to prayerfully consider committing your life to God, but I'm sure she'll remind you of her terms before you leave tomorrow morning."

Chapter Twenty-Four

When Sarah left the *daadi haus*, she breathed deeply in the chilly night air. The stars overhead reminded her of the night she and Jakob had ridden home together. She wrapped the thrill of that night around her as she hugged herself. All her hopes and dreams about a future with Jakob had seemed to be coming true then. Now she had no idea what he thought of her. Since Rebecca had confessed and Herman had revealed his identity, she could at least tell Jakob the whole story. And reassure him his sister wouldn't be on TV.

Knowing Jakob, he would forgive her quickly and easily, but would he ever trust her again?

When she entered the kitchen, Jakob sat on the bench on her brother's side of the table, where he used to sit when he visited Lydia. A pain so sharp and sudden shot through Sarah, she gasped.

"Are you all right?" Jakob jumped up, setting the bench rocking. He held it with one hand so it wouldn't tip over, but he kept his attention on Sarah.

"I'll be fine." She couldn't tell him the agony she'd endured whenever he came to visit Lydia. Or was that keeping secrets again? Maybe she could try to be more honest. "Actually, seeing you there reminded me of when you studied for baptismal classes—with Lydia."

Jakob winced, and Sarah stopped talking. Why had she hurt him like that?

When he opened his eyes, he avoided looking at her. "I remember you being there."

"Right," Sarah said. "Because I fixed your favorite desserts."

"You were always so thoughtful, caring about other people more than yourself."

So maybe he hadn't realized she'd had a crush on him. Sarah breathed more easily. "I think we have apple pie, if you'd like some."

Jakob smiled. "When have I ever turned down dessert?"

"Never, as far as I know." Sarah got out a plate and fork, and then cut Jakob a generous slice.

"Aren't you going to have any?" he asked after she set the plate in front of him.

"I'd better not. My stomach is churning."

"Not because of me, I hope."

Sarah waved a hand to dismiss that. "So many things have happened today. My stomach feels as if I've been twirled around until I'm dizzy. A lot like the way I used to feel when I was small and you took my hands and spun me in a circle until neither of us could walk straight."

Jakob smiled at the memory. "I'd end up so dizzy, I'd collapse onto the ground. Then we'd both stagger around for a while."

"Yes, that's exactly how I feel right now."

"I'm sorry. It's not pleasant when you're an adult."

No, it wasn't. And it had been made worse by the memory of Lydia and the worry over what Jakob had come to say. Sarah lowered herself onto the bench opposite him. "You said you wanted to talk?"

"I do, but I don't know where to start. When I came here the first time tonight, it was because I'd heard something disturbing at the meeting, and I wanted to ask you about it. It was late, but you and Rebecca seem to be working long hours recently, so I hoped you might still be awake. Then things happened, and I made a fool of myself."

"No, you didn't," she assured him.

As if he hadn't heard her, Jakob continued, "I owe you an apology. For so many things. First of all, for barging in on you and your guests." He rubbed his forehead. "I saw the open door and feared for your *mammi*'s safety. I went to pull it shut and heard men's voices. My first thought was that she was in danger, so I raced down the hall and..."

"And I was with Herman," Sarah said in a monotone. "I'm sorry you saw that. He caught me off guard when he grabbed me unexpectedly. Otherwise it never would have happened."

Jakob cut a bite of pie, forked it into his mouth, and chewed slowly. "Delicious, as always," he said after he swallowed. "I know that, Sarah. I was so startled to see you there, when I was expecting your grandmother or possibly robbers or something, I said some stupid things. Then I was so embarrassed and upset with myself, I hurried away. I want to apologize."

"You don't need to."

"Yes, I do. I blurted out some things I shouldn't have. And I accused you of lying before even knowing the circumstances. Will you forgive me? And please forget everything I said in the heat of the moment."

"Of course, I forgive you, if you'll forgive me." But forget everything he said? Including the part about dating?

"There's nothing to forgive, Sarah."

She hung her head. "You haven't heard my story yet, but you said you came over to ask me something."

"Oh, right." Jakob concentrated on cutting another bite of pie and avoided her eyes. "It seems rather foolish now, and I wish I hadn't listened to idle gossip, but when they mentioned my sister…"

Sarah steeled herself for what was coming. Had someone found out about the TV show? What if Abner had bragged about what he'd done?

Jakob forked another bite of pie into his mouth. Then after what seemed like an extra-long wait, he spoke. "Someone mentioned that Rebecca had been spotted at Yoder's barn on Friday night. I insisted she'd spent the evening with you, but this person was equally as insistent she was there."

Sarah wished she had a piece of pie in front of her to avoid answering his unspoken question. "I take it you haven't been home since the meeting?"

"No, I came straight here. Why?"

"If you had, Rebecca might have answered your question."

"Actually, my first thought was to come here. I'd believe your answer. Lately I haven't been so sure about my sister."

"This should probably come from Rebecca. It's her story to tell."

"Wait, the way you're talking it sounds as if…"

Sarah stood. "It's a long story, but first I'd like something to drink. Lemonade, root beer, or milk?

"Root beer, please, but what's going on?"

"Give me a minute." Sarah took her time pouring a glass of root beer for each of them and then returned to the bench. She slid a glass across to Jakob and clenched a hand around her own cup, struggling to find the best way to tell the whole story.

Jakob took a sip but eyed her warily over the rim of the glass.

"If you'd gone home tonight, you would have heard. Rebecca confessed to your parents earlier this evening."

"Confessed what? Are you trying to tell me she was at the barn?"

"There's more to it than that. Maybe I should start at the beginning with my part in the whole confession."

"You're scaring me." He set his glass down with a bang. "Are you telling me you were involved with this too?"

"Oh, Jakob, I made a foolish mistake, and it affected so many people." Sarah recounted the parachute falling from the sky and her rescue of Herman. "I thought I was doing a good thing, but instead I…"

"I promised myself I wasn't going to ask about the two men, but it's been eating away at me."

"I'll explain more about them as I go on, but Herman was the one claiming to have a broken leg, and Paul—the one who gave you all that money—arrived to help him."

"Claiming? He really didn't have one?"

"We didn't find that out until later. Much later." Sarah ran a finger around the rim of her glass and then continued telling him about her discovery of the men's true identities.

Jakob leaned forward, his eyes intent. "Did they have anything to do with the incident at the wedding?"

"Abner confirmed that Herman did."

"What does Abner have to do with this?"

Sarah sighed. "That's another facet of this mess."

A frown creased Jakob's forehead. "And Rebecca plays a part in it?"

"Yes, she does. Up until now, it was her story to tell, but because she's already told your parents, I hope she won't mind me telling you." Sarah took a sip of root beer to soothe her dry, tight throat. When she set it down, she told him about Rebecca slipping out the first time.

"But she was here when I came to get her."

"Yes, she must have just come in the back door."

"So you two really weren't working on lesson plans all that time?"

"I was, but Rebecca was out with Abner."

Jakob's fists clenched at the mention of Abner's name. "Then Amos wasn't mistaken about Abner's car being here that night." His voice was so sad, Sarah wanted to reach out and comfort him.

She nodded. "That was the first time."

"The first time?" Jakob's voice rose. "Please tell me she didn't go to the barn."

Swallowing hard, Sarah said, "I wish I could. I'm not going to tell you all that happened there—I'll leave that for Rebecca—but Herman had arranged for her and Abner to be filmed."

Jakob shaded his eyes with his hand and rubbed his forehead. His words heavy, he said, "And Rebecca agreed?"

"Oh, no, she had no knowledge of it. And I would never have known if I hadn't eavesdropped."

"You eavesdropped?" Jakob looked so startled, Sarah almost wished she hadn't mentioned it.

She bit her lip. No matter what, she'd tell the whole story, including all the parts that made her ashamed. Would Jakob want to have anything to do with her once she confessed everything? Taking a deep breath, she plunged into the part about overhearing Herman's conversation and warning Rebecca.

Relief filled Jakob's eyes. "So that's why you were so insistent on seeing Rebecca earlier today, isn't it?"

"Yes. I'm sorry I was so short with you when I was looking for her, but I worried she might go out with Abner before I could caution her about the filming."

"*Ach*, Sarah." He reached across the table and set a hand on hers.

Sarah's heart fluttered, and her spirit soared. The gentle pressure of his fingers on hers made her lose all sense of time and place. She'd never seen him be this affectionate with her sister. He'd always kept his distance with Lydia, and Emma used to mock the two of them for never touching, for Jakob's stiffness. Jakob had never been that way with Sarah when they were young. He'd held her hand, put an arm around her.

Sarah closed her eyes and struggled to hold back the sadness flooding over her. Of course, this meant no more to Jakob than it did when they were children. He would have comforted Rebecca the same way.

"Are you all right?"

The tenderness and caring in Jakob's tone tore at Sarah's heart. She wanted so much more from him than he was willing to give. "I—I'll be fine." *Neh*, that was a lie. She'd never be fine as long as they were only friends.

"You've had quite a day, haven't you?" Jakob smoothed a finger over the back of her hand. The gentle soothing touch, the tenderness in his eyes touched a chord deep within Sarah's heart.

If only it meant as much to him as it did to her. Every nerve in her body tingled, and she struggled to come up with a coherent reply. "Actually it's been quite a few weeks," she managed to say. "And there's more I haven't told you."

At Jakob's raised eyebrows but sympathetic glance, Sarah lowered her eyes. She had to stop making a big deal about every innocent look and touch, but she tucked them away to dream about later. So far, he'd been gracious, but he'd only date someone "completely honest." She'd already failed that test.

Still, she needed to finish her story so Jakob would know the whole truth. Even if she was confessing too late.

"When *Dat* found out what the two men were doing, he insisted I ask them to leave. That's what I was doing when you showed up." She released her breath in a long sigh. "They agreed to go, but Paul insisted on paying for their stay. I'd refused the money, but when he insisted, I thought it would help Ada's baby brother."

"That was wonderful," Jakob agreed. "Benefit sales make good money, but to have a huge sum to start makes it so much easier."

"Anyway, when I suggested you wait here in the kitchen, I planned to ask them to not show Rebecca's film. God answered my prayer, and Herman agreed. He's going to redo his show using actors." Sarah couldn't help getting a little teary-eyed. "I'm so relieved for Rebecca. She doesn't know yet. When you go home tonight, you can tell her and your parents."

"That's wonderful *gut* news. I'm sure the whole family will be thrilled." Jakob flashed her a brilliant smile. "Thank you for doing that."

"It was the least I could do, because I was the one who invited them here in the first place."

Jakob nodded, then he gazed off into the distance, and his eyes grew sad. "I can't believe you kept all this from me. We've been best friends since we were little. I thought you trusted me enough to be honest."

"I do trust you." But their relationship had eroded when Jakob started courting Lydia. How could she trust the only man she'd ever loved when he planned to marry another woman? And Jakob had avoided her since the breakup.

"I wanted to tell you, but I'd promised Rebecca," Sarah said.

"A promise to my sister is more important than being honest with me?"

"Oh, Jakob, I've been so *ferhoodled*, I couldn't tell right from wrong, lies from truth. I'm still not sure what to do when I'm asked to keep a secret that harms other people. I made a promise and kept my word, but maybe Kyle was right when he said, 'Some promises are meant to be broken.'"

"He may be right about that, if people are being hurt. It's hard to decide when you have two conflicting principles, and you're trying to uphold both."

Jakob understood and believed the best of her! Relief washed over her. "Oh, Jakob, that's exactly how I felt the whole time." But just because he understood, it didn't mean she'd ever meet his high standards. Could he possibly forgive her failings? That might be too much to ask, but at least he hadn't judged her too harshly. "I'm so glad all these secrets are out in the open, and I can be honest about everything."

Or at least most things. Her feelings for Jakob remained a closely guarded secret. For a brief moment, Sarah wondered what would happen if she told that secret too, but she wasn't ready to risk their newfound friendship. Perhaps someday she'd be brave enough to share even this secret.

"Speaking of secrets," Jakob said, "I've always admired your loyalty and your ability to keep a secret, even at great cost to yourself. You kept plenty of mine when we were younger. When you fell in the creek and tore your dress, you never mentioned I was the one who'd talked you into it."

Sarah smiled. "I didn't want you to get in trouble."

"And that's why you kept Rebecca's secret too, isn't it?"

Sarah nodded. "I don't ever want to be the cause of anyone getting hurt."

"That's one of the things I love about you."

Jakob's smile melted her heart. And he'd used the word *love.* No, he hadn't said *I love you,* but *things I love about you* was close enough to send her pulse skittering.

"Sarah, I'll be honest with you. My first thought when I saw you with that man was that you had fallen for an *Englischer.*"

Like Lydia. He hadn't said that, but it must have reminded him of her sister's betrayal.

"It upset me so much, I couldn't stay. But as I was driving away, I knew I'd misinterpreted the situation, and I had to come back to apologize. Will you forgive me for misjudging you?"

"Certainly. And as long as we're apologizing, I wanted to explain about Saturday. I'd told you I'd be going visiting with my family, and I intended to do that. That morning, though, *Mammi* worried the men were planning something. I couldn't leave her alone, so I stayed home."

"But that wasn't safe. I wish I'd known. I would have stopped and offered protection."

Was he thinking of her as a little sister again? "It was good I stayed. We did thwart Herman's plans, although I have no idea what they were. He called and cancelled them."

"If something like that ever happens again, please let me know. I don't like to think of you dealing with a dangerous situation alone."

"As *Mammi* always reminds me: our lives are in God's hands, so there's no need to fear."

Her grandmother was right about that, as always. And after spending time with Herman, Sarah appreciated being around Jakob, who shared the same assurance, the same comfort, and the same faith. If only they could share one other thing—their love.

Chapter Twenty-Five

As Sarah was getting ready for school in the morning, Paul pulled the rental car into the driveway of the *daadi haus*. He went inside and came out a few minutes later, carrying the duffel bag over his shoulder and the battery box in his hands. While he set them in the trunk, she hurried down to the kitchen, packed some cinnamon rolls, and headed out the door to catch them before they left.

After a quick knock, she walked in to find Herman standing beside the bed in his gray walking cast.

"Did you order me a wheelchair at the airport?" he demanded.

Paul nodded. "Once we arrive, we'll see if they think you need it."

"Of course, I need it. Look at me. I can barely stand, let alone hobble."

Mammi came downstairs. "Hmm, maybe you should have done more of that dancing."

Herman glared at her. "What would you know about it?"

"Nothing about dancing, but I do know it's hard to

get moving after lying around in bed for weeks. Exercise helps, though."

"*Mammi* had an emergency operation a few years ago," Sarah said. "And she helped my sister Emma recover after her car accident, so I'm sure she can give you good advice about getting back on your feet."

Paul and *Mammi* both smiled at Sarah's pun, but Herman's unpleasant expression didn't change.

"You want help getting out to the car?" Paul asked. "Or would you rather limp there by yourself?"

Herman tottered a few steps and grabbed for an end table to hold himself up. "If you were the one with the bum leg, you wouldn't think these attempts at humor were funny."

"Well, at least you picked a good place to rest." *Mammi* pointed to the open Bible on the table. "I hope that means you intend to keep your promise."

"Promise?" Herman stared at her blankly.

"I think we agreed you'd pray about getting right with God." *Mammi* gave him an encouraging smile. "Reading a few verses before you leave would be a good start."

"Oh, right, yeah, yeah, I'll think about it once I get back. We'll get that *Homespun Wisdom* show on the road. Already pitched it and got a good response, so we need to tape you in action so they can see how awesome the idea is."

"If you've already put that in motion, you'd better get moving on your part of the bargain."

"Oh, and I have a designer working on the cross-stitch logo for the show. Getting *Bonnet Rippers* off the ground will take most of my time when I return, but I'll keep moving ahead on this, don't you worry."

"I'm not worried in the least," *Mammi* said, "except about the condition of your soul."

Herman gave her a sickly smile. "Yes, well, we'd better get going so we're not late." He staggered to the doorway and leaned against the wall.

Paul said, "Why don't you keep going while I say my good-byes? I suspect I'll still beat you to the car unless you change your mind about needing help."

"I can do it," Herman growled.

As soon as he started down the hall, Paul turned to them. "When I get home, I plan to start going to church."

Mammi's approving smile lit up her face. "That's a good first step. I have a gift for you."

Paul shook his head. "No, we're the ones who are indebted to you."

Moving to the end table Herman had leaned on, *Mammi* picked up the Bible. "Take this with you. I'm sure you'll find it helpful. And if Herman decides to keep his end of the bargain, it'll come in handy."

"I can't take your Bible," Paul protested, but *Mammi* persisted until he tucked it under his arm and promised to read it on the flight home.

"We'll walk you out to the car," *Mammi* said, "but do you know the Saul-Paul story from the Bible? Saul was persecuting Christians, but after a light came down from heaven and God spoke to him, he realized the error of his ways. Paul became a great man of God. I'll pray that God will transform you in the same way."

"Thank you for your prayers. And years ago my grandma told me that story, but I'd forgotten it."

"Seems it's time to remember a lot of the things she taught you."

"I intend to. Thank you for putting me on the right path again." Paul reached out and shook *Mammi*'s hand.

"That wasn't my doing; it was God's," *Mammi* said.

Paul smiled. "You're right." Then he turned to Sarah and extended his hand. "And thank you for being a godly example."

"Oh, but I wasn't. I lost my temper and said so many things I shouldn't have. I—"

Paul interrupted. "We deserved it. And you were honest about how you felt. Sometimes speaking your mind is important too."

They reached the porch as Herman was inching his way down the few stairs by gripping the handrail, pivoting on his good leg, and hopping to the next step.

"A walking cast means you can step on it," Paul said.

"I'm not taking a chance."

Paul opened the car door for him, then rounded the car and got in the driver's seat. He set the Bible on the passenger seat. "Don't blame me if we're late."

"You were the one who spent all your time inside talking," Herman said.

"But who's holding us up now?"

"What's this?" Herman grumbled, pointing to the thick black book.

Paul grinned. "Reading material for the plane."

With an annoyed look, Herman picked up the Bible and plunked it down on the center console between the seats. Then grasping his cast on each side of his leg, he swiveled into place and set his leg down.

"I'll be praying," *Mammi* said as Paul put the car in gear.

"We both will," Sarah added.

Paul beamed at both of them. "We'd appreciate that."

Mammi turned to Sarah as the car turned into the street. "It certainly seems God brought them into our lives for a reason."

"You're right, *Mammi*. Knowing Paul is interested in spiritual things makes everything that happened worthwhile. I'd better head off to school, but when I get home in the afternoon, I'll have Zeke and Abe help me disassemble the bed and put it in the shed."

"You do that," *Mammi* said, "so it'll be ready for the next person God brings our way."

Sarah only hoped that person wouldn't drop from the sky, although she had to admit, God had turned this situation into a gift from above.

Eager to get to school and see Rebecca, Sarah raced inside, grabbed her satchel, and hurried through the fields. When she arrived, Rebecca's face looked pale and drawn, but her smile was radiant.

"I'm so glad I told *Mamm* and *Dat*," she said. "I feel so much better. Thank you for being such a supportive friend, Sarah. I can't tell you how much that means to me."

Sarah took her lunch out of her satchel and set it beside Rebecca's. "You look tired this morning, though."

"I didn't sleep well last night," Rebecca admitted. "I kept dreaming my private life was appearing on TV, so nightmares kept me awake most of the night."

"You didn't see Jakob?"

Rebecca shook her head. "We were all asleep when he came home last night, and he went in to take care of *Dat* really early, and they talked for a long while. I left before he came out for breakfast."

"Then you don't know the news?"

"What news?"

Sarah glanced at the clock. The scholars would be arriving in a few minutes, but she could at least give her friend a quick account. "*Dat* insisted I ask Paul and Herman to leave, which they did this morning. But I also told them I didn't think it wasn't legal to use you on TV without your consent. Herman argued at first, but in the end, they agreed not to use your film. They went back home to start casting the TV show with actors instead of real people."

Rebecca grabbed Sarah's arm so tightly, fingernails dug into her skin. "Are you sure?"

"I'm positive. I heard Herman on the phone giving the orders."

Her friend's eyes widened. "You were eavesdropping again?"

Sarah laughed. "I guess I was. But he knew I was in the room."

"You're really serious?"

"*Jah*, Rebecca, he told them to use your segment to show the actors what to do. Some people will see it, but it won't be on TV."

Squealing, Rebecca jumped up from the desk and threw her arms around Sarah. She was hopping around, hugging Sarah, when the first scholar arrived. She let go and stood demurely by her desk while Sarah went to the door to greet the children. She couldn't keep the huge grin from her face, though. Every time Sarah looked at Rebecca, she smiled so broadly, the skin around her eyes crinkled.

The two of them shared smiles all day long, and after the last child had left the schoolhouse, Rebecca's eyes were misty. "I was so thrilled this morning that I never even thanked you."

"No need to thank me. I'm relieved this is over and I could fix the mistakes I caused."

"But you didn't do anything to deliberately hurt anyone or disobey the way I did. For me, this truly is a gift of God's mercy." Rebecca picked up her satchel. "Oh, Sarah, thank you for being such a wonderful *gut* friend. I can't wait to get home to tell *Mamm* and *Dat*." She rushed from the schoolhouse, and Sarah, her heart light, strolled through the cornfields enjoying the beauty of nature and the peace in her soul.

Chapter Twenty-Six

After school the next day, Rebecca turned to Sarah. "I know I shouldn't ask for a favor after all you've done for me, so feel free to say no." Rebecca stared off into the distance for a few minutes. "Abner wants to get together and talk. I think he plans to apologize."

Sarah held up her hand. "I'd like to help you, but you can't meet at my house. I promised your parents."

"That wasn't what I was going to ask. I intend to follow my parents' rules. I told Abner I could only meet him in my living room with someone there to chaperone. He's not happy about that."

Sarah was, though. At least Rebecca would be safe.

"Actually, neither am I. I don't want my parents and Jakob listening to what Abner and I say to each other, so I wondered if you'd be our chaperone."

"Me?" Sarah didn't want to hear her friend's private conversation. "Your parents said they needed to chaperone."

"I know *Mamm* would let you do it. She trusts you." *What if I don't want to do it?* "I don't think—"

"Please, Sarah. I trust you more than anyone I know.

You'd never gossip or tell anyone what you hear. And with you there, I think I'd have the courage to break up with him. I can't do that with my parents listening in."

How could Sarah refuse? "If your parents agree, I'll do it to support you."

"Thank you. This means the world to me. Could you come after dinner tonight?"

Sarah nodded, dread pooling in the pit of her stomach. She wished she could avoid going. She disliked confrontations and seeing people get hurt.

This time when she and Rebecca went their separate ways, Sarah slogged along. The whole way home she prayed for strength and wisdom, and she continued asking for guidance as she walked to the Zooks' house after dinner.

Jakob answered the door, and again she found herself tongue-tied as she stared at him.

He held up a hand. "Let me guess. You're here to see my sister." He twisted his mouth into an exaggerated pout.

Sarah giggled at his comical expression. "Actually I am."

He opened the door and stepped aside so she could enter. "I'm wounded, but I know you'd much rather spend time with Rebecca than me."

"Oh, no, that's not true." Sarah said it so forcefully, her cheeks burned.

He perked up. "Really?"

To hide her embarrassment, she said, "I enjoy spending time with both of you."

"In that case, may I drive you home tonight?"

Before she could stop herself, a wide grin stretched across her face.

"Is that a *yes*?"

Although she longed to shout her answer, she only nodded. She concentrated on taking off her coat so he couldn't see the excitement in her eyes.

"I'll look forward to it," he said quietly as Rebecca charged into the hallway.

"Oh, good, you're here." Rebecca took Sarah's coat and hung it on a peg. "I know you didn't want to do this."

Jakob, who had started walking down the hall, turned to his sister. "If you knew she didn't want to do it, then why are you making her?"

Hands on her hips, Rebecca stared him down. "It's not your business."

Ignoring her, Jakob said to Sarah in a gentle voice, "If it makes you uncomfortable, you don't have to do it."

"Jakob!" Rebecca's tone was shrill.

Sarah smiled at Jakob. His caring about her welfare touched her. "It's all right. I promised to do it, and I will."

"Is this one of those promises that need to be broken?"

"Stop it, Jakob!" Rebecca grabbed Sarah's arm and dragged her past Jakob and down the hall. "I need Sarah's help." When she got to the living room doorway, she let go of Sarah's arm and shooed her brother away. "I thought you had another committee meeting tonight about the Rupp baby's benefit sale."

"I do." Jakob glanced at the grandfather clock in the hallway. "I'll be leaving soon." His eyes were serious as he looked at Sarah. "If you really don't want to be here, I can take you home now."

Sarah would have liked to take him up on his offer—

both to escape the upcoming confrontation and to spend time alone with him, but Rebecca needed her. "Thanks, but I'll stay here."

Was that disappointment in his eyes or only wistful thinking on her part?

As soon as Jakob left, Rebecca clutched Sarah's arm again. "I was so afraid you might not come."

Sarah detached her arm from her friend's grip and settled in a chair in the far corner of the room, wishing she could disappear altogether.

"Oh, Sarah," Rebecca wailed, "this is going to be so difficult. I still love him, but I'm not sure I can trust him."

How can you have love without trust? Sarah opened her mouth to say that but swallowed back the words. Rebecca had gotten upset the last time Sarah had questioned her relationship with Abner. Better to listen and not comment.

Rebecca paced from one end of the room to the other. "I'm so nervous. I have no idea what to say to him."

"Why don't we pray?" Sarah suggested.

The two of them bowed their heads, and when Rebecca lifted her head, some of the worry lines around her eyes had eased.

A few of the lines reappeared when someone knocked on the door. Rebecca sucked in her breath. "He's here. I can't do this, Sarah." She rushed into the hall and returned with Abner.

His mouth opened when he saw Sarah sitting in the corner of the room. He gave Rebecca a *what-is-she-doing-here?* look, and she shrugged.

"*Mamm* insisted we need a chaperone. I thought Sarah would be better than my parents or brother."

"I guess. But we don't need a chaperone."

Rebecca gave him a sideways glance.

"Aw, come on, Bec. I already apologized for that." Abner plodded over to the couch and sat down. He patted the cushion next to him, but Rebecca sat in a nearby chair.

Rebecca frowned at the disgust on his face. "Sitting in separate places is another rule my parents set when they heard about the other night."

"You told your parents?" Abner leaned so far forward Sarah worried he'd pitch onto his face. "I can't believe you'd do that."

"I told them everything, including about the filming."

Abner groaned and covered his face. "So I guess they don't trust me now."

Did they ever? For sure and certain, Jakob never had.

"I'm not sure I do either." Rebecca's voice was calm and steady, but hurt flickered in her eyes.

Abner's head snapped up, and he stared at her. "You don't mean that, Bec. You can't. I said I was sorry and promised never to do it again."

"I want to believe that, but…"

"But what? What else do I have to do to prove it to you? Tell me and I'll do it."

"I've already told you. Join the church."

"I already promised I would."

Sarah sighed inwardly. A marriage built on one person's faith had a shaky foundation. In time Abner might come to resent joining the church if he did it to please Rebecca rather than out of a true commitment to God.

Rebecca pinched her lips together, and Sarah knew her friend well enough to know she was holding back tears. Her voice quavered as she said, "I think we should stop seeing each other until baptismal classes begin."

"But that's not until spring. I can't be apart from you that long." Abner held out his arms, but Rebecca shrank back in the chair.

"You asked what you could do to regain my trust."

"Six whole months apart? You can't mean it. I'll give you a few days to think it over."

"No, Abner."

He slumped forward, elbows on his knees, his face in his hands, his shoulders shaking. "You're the only one I have. My family…my job… You know what they're like…" His voice broke.

Sarah's heart ached for him. She understood why Rebecca believed he needed her. Sarah tuned out the rest of the conversation and spent her time in prayer for both of them. By the time she lifted her head, Abner was rushing from the room, an anguished look on his face, and Rebecca was rocking back and forth in the chair, eyes closed, one hand covering her mouth, her shoulders shaking. Sarah was torn. Should she go to her friend to comfort her or give her some time alone?

A strangled sob came from Rebecca's lips. "That was one of the hardest things I've ever done. I know it was the right thing to do, but it hurts so much."

Sarah crossed the room and sat near Rebecca. "I'm sorry it was painful. You were very brave to do it."

"I don't think he believed me until I returned the cell phone."

So Abner was the one who'd given her the phone. Sarah hadn't seen her hand it to him, so that must have happened while she prayed. "Maybe realizing you meant it will encourage him to make some changes in his life."

Jakob walked past the living room and stopped when he saw them. "As I was coming in, I ran into Abner dashing to his car. He didn't even greet me. I hope that means you two broke up."

Rebecca sniffled. "I thought we needed to."

"Good job, little sis." Jakob's tone was light and teasing, but admiration shone on his face.

Rebecca made a face. "I'm not little."

"You are to me." Jakob reached down and patted her on the shoulder. "No matter how old you get, you'll still be younger."

"Ooh, you." Rebecca batted his hand away. "And is Sarah a little sister too?"

"Not exactly."

"But she's two years younger than me."

"Sarah's different. She's more mature, for one thing." He jumped back to evade Rebecca's elbow. "But I must say, you acted mature tonight."

Rebecca ducked her head, but not before Sarah caught a glimmer of smile shining through the tears.

"I know it wasn't easy, but you did what was right," Jakob said.

"Why does doing right hurt so much?"

Sarah wished she had an answer that would satisfy her friend. When people were hurting, they often resented others telling them it would all work out for good. Sometimes it was better to listen and let them discover that truth for themselves at a later date.

"Will you be all right?" Sarah asked.

Rebecca nodded. "I'll cry my heart out in bed tonight, but I'll survive." She turned to Jakob. "You'll take Sarah home, won't you?"

"I already told her I would."

"Oh." Rebecca glanced from one to the other, her eyebrows raised. Then she said to Sarah, "Thank you for being here. I'll see you tomorrow."

"I'll be praying," Sarah assured her.

While they were putting on their coats, Jakob asked, "How are you? I'm sure it wasn't easy having to listen to someone's breakup."

"Breakups are never easy," Sarah replied. As he would know.

Chapter Twenty-Seven

Sarah and Jakob walked in silence to the buggy, marveling at the stars and the full moon, a glowing orange circle.

As the horse trotted off, Jakob asked, "Do you want to talk about what happened tonight?"

Sarah would love to, but she couldn't. "I wouldn't feel right about that. It's Rebecca and Abner's choice if they want to tell."

"You and your secrets," Jakob said. "Maybe someday you'll trust me enough to tell me all your secrets."

His tone was teasing, but Sarah answered seriously. "I do trust you enough, but when people confide in me, I don't feel right telling anyone else unless I have their permission."

Pulling gently on one rein, Jakob guided the horse to turn left at the corner. "Your friends are very blessed. I hope someday I'll be lucky enough to be counted among them."

"What?" she said indignantly. "You already are. We've been friends for as long as I remember."

He waited until the horse had completed the turn

before looking at her thoughtfully. "I must say you're a generous soul to still call me a friend after the way I've treated you for the past few years."

"That was understandable, given the circumstances. You were hurting."

"Yes, I was, although not in the way most people think."

When she turned puzzled eyes toward him, he glanced away. "That's a story for another time."

"Are you concealing secrets from me?" she demanded with mock sternness.

"Could be," he said, his eyes fixed on the road ahead.

"And whose confidences are you keeping?"

"Only my own." His words held a tinge of sadness.

Sarah longed to ask if he'd trust her enough to tell her someday, but she suspected if he did, his revelations would be equally as painful for her as for him. The past few weeks she'd learned that honesty made life so much easier and lifted a lot of burdens. But was she ready for that honesty?

And what about the secret she'd harbored for years, the secret she'd kept in her heart since early childhood? Was she living a lie by pretending to feel friendship for Jakob when she was so deeply in love with him? Didn't he deserve to know the truth? But could she bare her heart and soul? How would he react if she did? Would she lose his friendship forever?

Jakob spoke, startling her from her internal argument. "You're quiet tonight. Another secret?"

Sarah nodded. A huge one.

The corners of Jakob's mouth lifted in an endearing smile. "Are you going to tell me?"

Sarah lowered her eyes. What if she told him and

spoiled their friendship? Would they go back to the years when he avoided her, turning away whenever she came near? Sarah ached inside to think about it.

"Sarah?" Jakob's kind tone invited her to share her deepest thoughts and feelings.

"Jakob, can I be honest with you?"

Without a second of hesitation, he answered, "Of course. I hope you'll always be honest with me."

"I should share this secret with you, but I'm afraid if I do, it'll spoil our friendship. I enjoy being with you, and I couldn't bear to lose our fun times together. I wouldn't want to go back to…" Her voice quavered, and she couldn't finish her sentence.

His voice rough, Jakob said, "You mean when I was so cruel, cutting you off and avoiding you?"

She nodded.

"I'm so sorry I did that. I let my shame blind me to your feelings." Jakob's raspy words revealed the depth of his pain. "That's a secret I need to share with you sometime, after you've shared yours. But will you forgive me for the way I treated you?"

"Of course." Sarah turned to face him on the seat. She wanted him to know she sympathized with him both then and now. "I knew you were hurting, and I understood."

"There's so much you don't understand, though." Jakob transferred the reins to his other hand and rubbed his forehead. "But back to your question. Nothing you say will affect our friendship. Even if what you say hurts or upsets me, I promise not to cut you off like that ever again."

The only sounds in the still night were the clip-clop

of the horse's hooves and the metal wheels hitting asphalt.

Sarah took a deep breath. "You're sure?"

Jakob turned to her with hurt in his eyes. "Sarah, I think you know me well enough to know I keep my word."

She hung her head. "That wasn't what I was questioning. I worry that telling you this will make you too uncomfortable to be around me."

"I've made my promise, so let's hear your secret."

Under the blankets Sarah clutched her hands together. She had no idea how to begin. Maybe she could ease into it by talking about their childhood. "Remember when you helped me with the kitten?"

"You mean when we were little?"

"*Jah.* You became my hero that day, and I had a huge crush on you."

Jakob's eyes softened, and his face relaxed into a grin. "Aw, I always thought you were sweet on me back then. If it makes you feel better, I felt the same."

"Really?" Sarah glanced up to see if he was joking, but his face was serious.

"Didn't you ever wonder why I skipped playing with my friends to spend time with you? I took a lot of teasing for it, but it was worth it. I thought you were the sweetest girl I'd ever met. Actually, I still think that." His teasing grin was back.

It was hard not to smile back, but if she did the conversation might get off track. "So back to my story. The more time we spent together, the more my feelings grew. I'm not sure exactly when I fell in love with you."

Jakob sucked in a breath.

"I only know I loved you more with each passing year until—"

"Until?" he prompted, a frown wrinkling his brow.

But Sarah couldn't go on. Memories she'd buried came rushing back, washing over her in a flood of agony.

"Until?" Jakob repeated.

"Until I had no right to." But even then, she kept right on loving him, knowing how wrong it was. She'd tried to tamp down those feelings, to think of him as a brother, but it hadn't worked.

He groaned. "Oh, Sarah, I've made such a mess of things." He pulled the buggy off to the side of the road and buried his head in his hands. "Can you ever forgive me for being such a fool?"

Sarah longed to comfort him but had no idea what he meant.

"You loved me all that time? I loved you, too, back then. All I thought about was waiting until you were old enough to ask you to marry me. But then…"

Then he fell for Lydia. And her world came crashing down.

A car roared up behind them, revving its engine and tailgating the buggy. At the first opportunity, Jakob pulled onto a wide part of the shoulder to let the driver pass. Sarah studied his profile, silhouetted in the moonlight. He was so close she could reach out and run her finger from his broad forehead down his cheek to stroke his strong jawline and clean-shaven chin. How handsome he'd look with a beard! Except it would mean he was marrying someone else, not her.

Then he turned and met her eyes, and she sucked

in a breath, and every nerve tingled. His dark eyes reflected starlight as he reached out and untangled her hands from the blanket. His hands closed over hers, gentle and comforting. He leaned toward her, his eyes burning, intense. "I need to know one thing: Could you ever care for me like that again?"

Sarah started to shake her head. No, she couldn't. Because every day she loved him more.

He winced, and his hands tightened on hers for a second before he let go. His lips pinched, he turned away. "I see," he said stiffly.

Ach, no, he misinterpreted what she meant. "Jakob?" she said softly. "I didn't shake my head because I don't care about you."

He glanced sideways at her, doubt clouding his eyes.

"I, I…" Sarah stared down at her clenched hands, pale against the navy woolen blanket tucked across her lap. "The truth is—" she paused to steady her breathing and her voice "—I never stopped loving you. The feelings I had for you back then have only grown stronger."

"Really?" His deep bass voice had grown husky.

When she nodded shyly, his face lit up. "You don't know how happy that makes me." Then he reached for her hands again and swallowed hard. "I've been trying to work up the courage to ask if I could court you. I didn't know if you'd ever consider it."

"You want to court me?" Sarah stared down at their entwined hands. "Thank you for the honor."

"But—?" Jakob's jaw tensed.

Sarah could barely push the words past her unyielding lips. "I'll never measure up to my sister, but I'll do my best."

"What?" Jakob's brows drew together. "I don't understand."

Sarah longed to reach out and smooth away the frown lines, but she resisted the urge. "You dated Lydia and hoped to marry her." She tried to keep her voice from wobbling but was unsuccessful. "I know I'm your second choice."

"Oh, Sarah, how could you believe—" Jakob shook his head. "I thought you knew. All along when I was courting Lydia, I—I was really attracted to you."

"Me?"

"I found myself being very judgmental and critical of Lydia. In the back of my mind, I was always comparing the two of you and finding Lydia lacking. I even asked her if she could be more like you."

"You did?"

"More than once." Jakob's cheeks flamed. "You were too young to court. I hoped I could transfer my feelings to Lydia because she looked so much like you. It didn't work."

"But you were upset when she turned you down."

"*Jah*, my pride was hurt." Jakob hung his head. "*Hochmut*. That's all it was." He looked away and then cleared his throat. "No, that wasn't the only reason."

Sarah longed to cover her ears. She couldn't bear to hear what he would say next. He claimed he'd cared for her more than Lydia, but she struggled to accept it.

"The real reason is that I was angry with myself for asking her when I didn't love her. I thought love would grow with time, but God saved us both from making a terrible mistake that night."

"Then why did you court her in the first place?"

Sarah sucked in a breath and held it while she waited for an answer. He took so long to respond, her lungs ached.

"I'm ashamed to admit this—" Jakob gazed off into the distance, his eyes troubled "—but I think I was drawn to her because she looked so much like you. I didn't realize it at the time, but now when I look back…"

Yet Jakob had shut her out of his life after his breakup with Lydia. "But you wouldn't even speak to me."

"Oh, Sarah." The anguish in Jakob's voice tore at her heart. "How could I face you after that? Realizing I was in love with—not the woman I was dating—but with her younger sister. Who was still too young for me. And who would never want to court me now that I'd courted her sister."

"You were in love with me then? I can't believe that—"

"Why not?"

"Because…because…" *Because it seems too good to be true. Because I never thought you'd ever love me. Because I'm not sure I'm worthy of your love.*

"Because why?" Jakob lifted her chin so he could look into her eyes.

The love shining in his eyes left Sarah breathless and tongue-tied. Tears sprang to her eyes.

"You've always been the only one for me." He slipped an arm around her shoulders and drew her closer. Then he lowered his head and pressed his lips to hers. His soft, tender kiss erased all doubts, and her eyes damp with tears, Sarah melted into his embrace. His lips conveyed his emotions, leaving her no doubt of his deep love.

"Oh, Jakob," she breathed when he pulled back and cupped her face in his hands. His fingers caressed her cheeks, and his eyes assured her of his devotion.

After they'd both caught their breath, Jakob cradled

her head against his shoulder. "I want you to know I never kissed Lydia or held her. I told her we needed to set an example for the other *youngie* because my father was the bishop, but the truth is I never felt about her the way I do about you."

Sarah drew back a little. "Maybe we should be setting an example too."

Jakob wrapped his arm around her again and pulled her close. "Umm, that's a good idea, but right now there's no one here to see us." He bent and claimed her lips again.

As the stars twinkled overhead, Sarah melted into his kiss, letting oceans of love flow over her, washing away old hurts and pain, until her heart felt weightless, soaring into the clouds. She had received a precious gift from above, one she would treasure the rest of her life: Jakob, her first—and only—true love.

* * * * *

Amish Recipes

With thanks to my Amish friends

Chicken Filling Casserole

4 eggs beaten
1½ c. cooked and diced chicken
3 c. chicken broth
1½ c. cooked diced potatoes (keep some water)
1 small onion chopped
1 c. diced celery
1½ c. milk
1½ tbsp. sugar
9 c. buttered and toasted bread cubes
Salt and pepper

Grease a 9 x 13 pan. Mix all ingredients together in a bowl and pour into pan. Bake at 350° for 1 hour.

Peanut Butter Delight

Crust
½ c. butter
1 c. flour
1 c. chopped pecans

Combine until a crumbly mixture. Put in a 9 x 13 pan and press. Bake at 350° for 20 minutes.

Peanut Butter Filling
8 oz. cream cheese
¼ c. milk
1 c. powdered sugar
1 c. peanut butter
8 oz. Cool Whip

Beat everything except Cool Whip until smooth. Fold in Cool Whip and spread over cooled crust.

Toppings
2 ¾ c. milk
1 box instant vanilla pudding
1 box chocolate instant pudding
8 oz. Cool Whip

Beat pudding mixes together with the milk. Spread over peanut butter layer. Spread Cool Whip on top. Garnish with chocolate chips. Refrigerate.

SPECIAL EXCERPT FROM

Love Inspired®

*Finally following his dreams of opening a bakery,
Caleb Hartz hires Annie Wagler as his assistant.
But they both get more than they bargain for when his
runaway teenage cousin and her infant son arrive.
Can they work together to care for mother and child—
without falling in love?*

Read on for a sneak preview of
The Amish Bachelor's Baby *by Jo Ann Brown,
available February 2019 from Love Inspired!*

"I wanted to talk to you about a project I'm getting started on. I'm opening a bakery."

"You are?" Annie couldn't keep the surprise out of her voice.

"Ja," Caleb said. "I stopped by to see if you'd be interested in working for me."

"You want to hire me? To work in your bakery?"

"I've had some success selling bread and baked goods at the farmers' market in Salem. Having a shop will allow me to sell year-round, but I can't be there every day and do my work at the farm. My sister Miriam told me you'd do a *gut* job for me."

"It sounds intriguing," Annie said. "What would you expect me to do?"

"Tend the shop and handle customers. There would be some light cleaning. I may need you to help with baking sometimes."

"Ja, I'd be interested in the job."

"Then it's yours. If you've got time now, I'll give you a tour of the bakery, and we can talk more about what I'd need you to do."

Gut." The wind buffeted her, almost knocking her from her feet.

She mumbled that she needed to let her twin, Leanna, know where she was going. He wrapped his arms around himself as another blast of wind struck them.

"Hurry…anna…" The wind swallowed the rest of his words as she rushed toward the house.

She halted midstep.

Anna?

Had Caleb thought he was talking to her twin? She'd clear everything up on their way to the bakery. She wanted the job. It was an answer to so many prayers, for God to let her find a way to help her sister be happy again, happy as Leanna had been before the man she loved married someone else without telling her.

Leanna was attracted to Caleb, and he'd be a fine match for her. Outgoing where her twin was quiet. A well-respected, handsome man whose *gut* looks would be the perfect foil for her twin's. But Leanna would be too shy to let Caleb know she was interested in him. That was where Annie could help.

As she was rushing to the house, she reminded herself of one vital thing. She must be careful not to let her own attraction to Caleb grow while they worked together.

That might be the hardest part of the job.

Don't miss
The Amish Bachelor's Baby *by Jo Ann Brown,*
available February 2019 wherever
Love Inspired® books and ebooks are sold.

www.LoveInspired.com

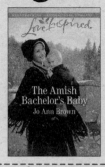

The Amish Bachelor's Baby
Jo Ann Brown

Save $1.00

on the purchase of ANY Love Inspired® book.

Available wherever books are sold, including most bookstores, supermarkets, drugstores and discount stores.

Save $1.00

on the purchase of ANY Love Inspired® book.

Coupon valid until April 30, 2019.
Redeemable at participating retail outlets in the U.S. and Canada only.
Limit one coupon per customer.

52616251

5 65373 00076 2 (8100)0 12411

® and ™ are trademarks owned and used by the trademark owner and/or its licensee.

© 2018 Harlequin Enterprises Limited

LICOUP45490

Annie was cleaning up the dishes when the phone rang. She
didn't recognize the number.

"Hello?"

"Annie, it's me."

Tyler.

Her estranged husband. The man she hadn't seen in two
years.

"Annie? You there?"

She shook her head. "Yes, I'm here. It's been a frazzling
day, Tyler. What do you want?"

A pause. "Something's happened last night, Annie. I can't
tell you everything, but the US Marshals are involved. I'm
being put into witness protection."

"Witness protection? Tyler, people in those programs have
to completely disappear."

In her mind, she heard Bethany ask when she would see
her daddy again.

"I know. It won't be forever. At least I hope it won't. I need to testify against someone. Maybe after that, I can go back to being me."

A sudden thought occurred to her. "Tyler, the reason you're going into witness protection… Would it affect me at all?"

"What do you mean?"

"Someone was following me today."

"Someone's following you?" Tyler exclaimed, horrified.

"You never answered. Could the man following me be related to what happened to you?"

"I don't know. Annie, I will call you back." He disconnected the call and went down the hall.

Marshal Mast was sitting at a laptop in an office at the back of the house. He glanced up from the screen as Tyler entered. "Something on your mind, Tyler?"

"I called my wife to tell her I was going into witness protection. She said she and my daughter were being followed today."

At this information, Jonathan Mast jumped to his feet. "Karl!"

Feet pounded in the hallway. Marshal Karl Adams entered the room at a brisk pace. "Jonathan? Did you need me?"

"Yes, I need you to make a trip for me. What's the address, Tyler?"

Tyler recited the address. Would Karl and Stacy get there in time? How he wished he could go with him…

Don't miss
Amish Haven *by Dana R. Lynn,*
available March 2019 wherever
Love Inspired® Suspense *books and ebooks are sold.*

www.LoveInspired.com

LISEXP0219

Love Inspired®

**Inspirational Romance to
Warm Your Heart and Soul**

Join our social communities to connect
with other readers who share your love!

Sign up for the Love Inspired newsletter
at **www.LoveInspired.com** to be the
first to find out about upcoming titles,
special promotions and exclusive content.

CONNECT WITH US AT:

Facebook.com/groups/HarlequinConnection

 Facebook.com/LoveInspiredBooks

 Twitter.com/LoveInspiredBks

LISOCIAL2018